MW01716963

Liberation

A Steamy Small-Town MMF Romance

Michele Lenard

CMFR

Contents

Chapter 1

Prologue

Prologue

The sexy stranger didn't seek me out before leaving town. After the look we shared I expected him to book an appointment, but he never showed, leaving little doubt that I'd ever see him again.

I'm disappointed, but not shocked. He and I exist in a world that isn't sure what to make of us, and sometimes that means pretending we're not different. It's one of the reasons I took this job at the spa, giving massages to tourists passing through town. I can be myself in front of strangers. Maybe even have a connection with them, albeit a brief one. It's better than nothing. And it protects my secret.

Living in a tiny resort town where everyone knows your name, your business, and what you had to eat that day, it's a rare feat to have any privacy. And yet, there are things I need to keep to myself, at least for now. I imagine my handsome stranger can relate to that.

He's part of a small crew that makes motocross videos, traveling the country for months on end to film in new places. It makes privacy even harder to come by for him than it is for me, which I guess is why I expected to see him again. If anyone can understand how a temporary connection with a stranger can be a lifeline that keeps you sane, I would've thought it'd be him.

Oh well. I suppose there will be other men. *Other tourists.* I just really liked the look of that one.

Chapter 2

Jace

I'd recognize those broad shoulders anywhere–I committed them to memory last month–and since then, I've been dreaming about what they'd look like under the shirt that hugs them. And that light brown hair with a hint of curl at the ends? God, how I want to thread my hands into it, and feel the silky strands glide between my fingers. My heart still races when I think about the way he looked at me–his steely gaze full of desire. What I'd give to feel that way again...

I wanted him right then and there, but years of masking my emotions kept my expression in check, and my body frozen in place. He was similarly guarded, and frankly, his gaze was the only hint of him being affected by my presence at all. But it was enough.

I'm not sure which of us broke the stare first, though I do remember shooting glances at each other for the rest of the afternoon. And when I rubbed my shoulder, sore from hoisting the camera around, he suggested a massage. To everyone else it was an offhand comment, a friendly offer. I knew better. It was an invitation to explore this thing between us. One I planned to take him up on, until our sponsors disrupted the schedule.

They sent us to Moab to film with some other riders, a task we barely completed since my best friend and star rider, Axel, had his mind stuck on his girl, Lennon. She wasn't his girl at the time, but he wanted her, and he went back to Katah Vista to claim her. I thought about going too, trying to find my sexy masseuse, Blake. But aside from that brief encounter at the bar, we didn't have any other contact, and I didn't want to come off as a stalker. So, Axel went to Katah Vista, and I went to Arizona to get ready for the first competition of the season.

I don't usually regret moving from one place to the next—traveling the world to film dirt bike videos and competitions with my best friend is a great life—but leaving without being able to act on the moment I shared with Blake made me feel sort of hollow. Like I was missing out on something that could've been great. Yeah, that's a weird thought to have after a simple look. Doesn't change the fact that I asked "what if" a few times. Now, I might finally get my chance.

Axel and Lennon decided to get serious and he moved there a few weeks ago. I thought about tagging along, but I scrapped the idea at the time. I didn't want to crowd them, and I didn't have much of a reason to return to Katah Vista beyond the single look from a sexy stranger. Fate seemed to have other plans, though, because here I am, sitting in this pub miles away from Katah Vista, and my sexy stranger happens to be sitting right in front of me. I'm not usually one to believe in such superstitions, but what else could it be? It can't be a coincidence. Unfinished business, maybe? Regardless, I won't waste my chance to explore whatever this is between us. Not again.

Standing over his shoulder, I speak just loud enough for him to hear me over the commotion of the busy restaurant. "Is this seat taken?"

He stiffens at the sound of my voice, turning slowly, as if he's unsure what he might find. Finally, I'm staring into the face I thought I might never see again.

Although I suspect we're close in age, Blake looks older. More man than boy, like he has to shave daily instead of once a week. It gives him a ruggedly handsome look compared to my boyishly attractive one.

His hazel eyes blink rapidly as he takes me in, confusion etched in his features. "You're..."

"Jace." I give him my hand.

"Blake." He takes it, and thick, strong fingers brushing against the back of my hand. The contact makes me shiver, and I swear I feel him do the same.

"I remember. May I?" I point to the barstool next to him. He nods, jaw shifting subtly as he fights a smile. *Does that mean he's happy to see me?*

The bartender sets a coaster in front of me before I can say anything else. "What can I get you?" he asks.

"What'd you get?" I ask Blake.

"A burger. And a pale ale." He lifts his glass, signaling that he'd like another.

"I'll have the same," I tell the bartender, who drifts off to place my order as I turn my focus back to the man beside me. His hazel eyes beam with a mixture of curiosity and anticipation. "What brings you to Utah? Vacation?" I ask.

"Work actually." He licks his lips before taking a sip of his beer, and I have to tear my eyes away before my mind can wander toward what else I'd like to see him do with his tongue.

"For the spa?"

"My other job. Or at least I think it will be."

I catch his eyes wandering down my body, and it makes my stomach flutter. *Damn, how long has it been since a look made me do that?* I swallow, trying to regain my focus. I vaguely remember him talking about teaching kids how to mountain bike. "The bike clinics?"

"You remember that?" The corner of his lip pulls up as he fights another smile. Without an audience he has to play a role for, he seems flattered, almost bashful. It's fucking adorable. I'm suddenly glad our first real opportunity to talk is here, away from people I suspect don't know this side of him.

"I remember."

"It's related to the bike clinics, yeah."

The bartender sets a beer in front of me, and I take a sip to wet my dry mouth. "So, you have two full-time jobs?"

"Most everyone in the valley does. There aren't many salary positions available and one hourly job doesn't pay the bills." A hint of red creeps into his cheeks. I hope he doesn't think I care about what kinds of jobs he has, or worse, his education. If I hadn't grown up riding with Axel, filming him along the way and establishing ourselves as sort of a package deal, I'm not sure where I'd be today.

"If it's so hard to make a living there, why do you stay?"

"I was born and raised there. Can't imagine living anywhere else." He gives a little shrug.

"Have you ever tried?" As soon as the words are out, I panic, wondering if they came across as negative. Fortunately, he doesn't seem to read into them.

"Yeah, actually. I did a few semesters of college in California years ago, and I learned I wasn't cut out to be a student or exist in a place where the only silence comes in the form of noise-canceling headphones."

The way he wrinkles his nose makes me chuckle. "You don't like the ocean?"

"I do. The best part about California was learning to surf, which is probably why I didn't make the best student. But I'm a mountain guy, through and through."

"You're tethered to Katah Vista, then?"

"For now. Maybe not forever, but if the outdoors is a part of you that's one of the few places I've found where you're truly surrounded by it."

I've traveled enough to know that's not true, but I understand the sentiment. Having spent a week there last month I know it's a special place, mainly because of the rugged beauty of the landscape. "So, Katah Vista is the best place to be, even if you have to work several jobs?"

"Especially then." His eyes light up as he talks about his hometown. "If you're willing to work a few jobs to live where you're happy it means you don't take that place for granted."

I feel myself nodding in agreement as the bartender sets our plates in front of us. "What's the other job, then?" I pop a fry in my mouth.

"It might be building a mountain bike park. Carter, the owner of the Katah Vista resort, thinks adding one will bring people in over the summer."

"I'm sure it would. The park here keeps the chairs spinning all summer. I didn't realize you built trails *and* taught people how to ride. How do you even have time for the spa thing?"

He finishes chewing with a tiny shake of his head. "I don't build trails. I help maintain them with the forest service, but I've never built one. I'm not even sure what my role would be if Carter decides to move forward with this idea. Right now, I'm just here to meet with a guy who's done this sort of thing before so we can better understand what it would take."

"Jackson Parker?"

Blake cocks his head to the side. "Yeah. How...?"

"There's some overlap between mountain biking and motocross. We sometimes film in the same areas so I end up meeting a lot of the riders. I'm actually here visiting Jackson myself. I scored a lift ticket off him so I could ride the bike park for a few days."

"They have motocross trails on the mountain?" His brows rise to his hairline, and I bite back another laugh. He's so *genuine*. It's refreshing.

"Nothing motorized on the mountain." I bump his leg under the bar, causing his eyes to dart briefly to mine. The trace of heat in them sends my pulse racing, but I force myself not to lean toward him. We are in pubic, and if my first impression is correct, he's not out. "Mountain bikes are a hell of a lot lighter than dirt bikes, and it's a nice change to ride something that doesn't weigh twice as much as I do. Plus, I needed a break from the guys. I love what I do and who I work with, but sometimes you need some space."

"I get that." The soft tone of his voice makes me think he really does.

"Yeah?" I can't stop the coy smile that tugs at my lip.

"Yeah. Although, now that I'm on a break from my little bubble, I'm realizing how much I like living in it."

"What do you mean?" I take a bite of my burger in an attempt to reign in my flirting.

"Well, sitting here—before you got here—I realized how much I like knowing people everywhere I go. It beats sitting alone for dinner."

"But you're not alone." I let that little challenge linger.

"Not anymore." Blake licks his lip again, and I swear I almost groan out loud.

I haven't been with a man in over a year, and while there have been plenty of women during that time, I've missed the weight of a male body against mine. The hard planes of a man's chest, stomach, and hips. The hint of scruff on his face at the end of the day. The big, strong hands sliding over my skin. My desire to experience those things has been present ever since I sat down, and while we've shared some great conversation, my body is growing impatient with all the talk.

Swallowing the last of my burger, I wipe my mouth and toss my napkin on the empty plate. "I think we should get out of here. Any chance I can convince you to come back to my room?

"I was sorta hoping you'd ask."

We each drop a few bills on the counter and head for the door.

Chapter 3

Blake

I brush my palms over my shorts, trying to rid them of the sweat gathering there. Jace's presence has me all sorts of anxious, like a friggin' horny teenager, and I kind of like it.

Confident without being cocky, the face of a young adult with the knowledge of a man, a shared love of things with two wheels—I can't pinpoint one specific thing that draws me to him. I just know I feel more alive in his presence.

My heart thrums erratically as our shoulders brush together, and I know if I stretch my hand out just slightly, I'd be able to reach his. I'm tempted, if only so I can feel the same jolt I did when we shook hands earlier. But that's a couple thing and we aren't one, no matter how familiar he already feels.

Destiny, fate, meant-to-be... When it comes to my love life, I've always assumed it'll unfold however it's supposed to. And since I was hopelessly drawn to Jace the first time I laid eyes on him, something I'd never experienced before, I wondered if maybe that was a sign. Then he left town abruptly, and I figured I was getting ahead of myself. That didn't stop me from fantasizing about him, though. So, finding him here, now, seems pretty significant. Especially since we've run into each other outside Katah Vista.

There are many things I love about my tiny hometown, but the dating scene isn't one of them, especially if you're bi and still in the closet. First off, there aren't an abundance of single people there year-round, let alone people with tastes like mine. Second, while I love small town life and the way everyone has each other's backs, I don't love the lack of privacy that comes with it. When people date or hook up it's big news, not because people are gossipy but because there's not much else to talk about in small towns.

Since my lifestyle is so different from what's considered "normal" it would definitely get tongues wagging, and I just haven't wanted to deal with that. Not that I think my interests would make me a pariah, but they might draw more attention than I want or need. So, I keep my preferences, and my affairs, to myself. Tourists are a great solution, letting me satisfy some basic needs without exposing my secrets. However, getting away from Katah Vista gives me the freedom to indulge in all sides of my personality. To find Jace here, where I don't have barriers, that's about as close to my definition of a miracle as you can get.

We reach the hotel—we're both staying in the same one, just two floors apart—and I follow Jace to his room. Pulling the key card from his back pocket, he swipes it over the sensor and steps inside, holding the door open just long enough for me to clear the threshold. As it swings shut, he presses me up against it, caging me between his arms.

My breath gets stuck in my lungs as I study his face, just inches from mine. Being roughly the same height, I can observe the thick brows resting over eyes that, up close, are more brown than black. His full lips are parted, and the dim light of the room reflects off the angles of his face. Despite being leaner that I am, Jace radiates strength, which seems barely contained as our chests brush against one another amid our heavy breathing. I reach up to touch his face, my calloused fingertips meeting the softest skin I've ever felt on a man. It's so smooth I doubt he's able to grow a full beard, which excites me more than I expected.

Jace closes his eyes, seeming to savor the feel of my touch, and my heart throbs deep inside my chest. Then without warning those dark eyes snap open and he presses his mouth to mine.

I barely have time to register how soft his lips are before his tongue slides inside, and a strangled groan rumbles from his throat. *Holy shit, that's hot.* I meet him head on, each of us fighting for dominance as lips and teeth and tongues clash.

Long, dexterous fingers slide through my hair, gripping the strands in a fist and giving a firm tug, tilting my head where he wants it. A tiny spark of pain mixed with pleasure shoots from the top of my head to my balls, and my cock starts to swell in my shorts. I reach around Jace's waist and pull him flush against my body, pressing our stiff cocks against one another. This time it's me who growls.

Hands tug at my shirt, lifting it up my chest, and before I realize it, mine are mimicking his. We break the kiss long enough to pull the fabric over our heads before crashing together again, a little less frenzied but no less intense.

Gripping Jace's ass, I hold him against me so our cocks get a little friction as we kiss each other senseless. Despite being eager to feel him instead of the fabric between us, I'm in no rush to end this kiss. I don't even remember the last time my lips touched someone else's, man or women, because let's face it, a hurried fuck at the end of a massage doesn't require it. The point is to get off, not make a connection, so I generally skip over this part. And I never really missed it, until now.

Jace's lips are unbelievably soft, even though nothing about his kiss is gentle. And the way he's panting, as if he needs air but is willing to sacrifice it to keep his mouth pressed to mine... Hot. As. Fuck.

Hands roam over my chest and down to my abs as he devours my mouth, making me dizzy with lust. My skin feels electric wherever he makes contact, and I swear if the wall wasn't holding me up my knees would buckle.

Fingertips trace the waistband of my shorts, sending a shiver up my back. When I feel them working the button open, I do the same, and seconds later our hard shafts are free, rubbing together.

Tingles shoot the length of my dick as the tip of his drags over me. I reach between us, trapping both our cocks in my fist, and give a firm squeeze as I tug. Jace pulls his mouth from mine and drops his head to my shoulder. "Fuuuccccckkk," he groans as I work us both. "I almost forgot how good it feels to have another cock rubbing against mine while I'm getting jerked off."

"I almost forgot how good it feels to hold another man's cock in my hand."

"I'm not going to last long if you keep doing this."

"Tell me you're prepared." I pump my hips gently, increasing the friction between us. "I didn't pack anything but condoms."

Jace lifts his head off my shoulder to look at me with a mischievous grin. "You didn't expect to get laid on your trip?"

"Not by a man in Utah."

He laughs, a sound I've never associated with sex but which somehow doesn't feel out of place. "A woman, then?" He arches a thick brow.

"Seemed more likely." I reach around with my free hand and cup his balls, rolling them between my fingers.

His head falls back with a contented little groan. "You're open to either, then?"

"I am."

"Me, too." He meets my gaze as his hips rock forward, grinding himself into my hand. "I haven't been with a man in ages, but I live out of my suitcase, I'm always ready." Fingertips graze over my hole, so lightly I'd think I imagined it if my hips didn't buck into my fist.

"Are you a top or bottom?" I nip at the plump bottom lip that's been taunting me all evening as my ass tries to seek out the finger teasing it.

"I'm good with both." He kisses me back. "But I haven't bottomed in a while."

"We'll take turns then. You should grab the lube." I swear he whimpers when I drop his cock to grab a condom from my wallet. As I roll it on, I watch him walk to his suitcase, his rigid length bobbing slightly with each step. Though slight for a man, lean with sinewy muscle, his dick is long and thick, and my mouth waters just looking at it. *Might have to taste him before the night's over.*

He sits at the end of the bed and tosses me a bottle, fisting his erection with a look that says *hurry up*. "Save enough for me to fuck you later."

Propping his feet on the mattress he leans back, slowing stroking his sex as he watches me move toward him. I squirt lube on my fingers and press them against his hole. It puckers from the cool gel, but relaxes as my fingers warm it up.

Between the slow, measured way his hand slides along his dick, and the glistening ring in front of me, I'm not sure where to look as I slip a finger inside. I settle on his hand, matching the pace of my finger to the rhythm he's setting. When the resistance starts to fade, I add another finger, stretching him as gently as I can.

As I work him Jace swivels his hips, straining to take me deeper. The sight of him laid out for me, eyelids fluttering closed in bliss, has my cock dripping with need from where it hangs heavily between my legs. I give it a quick tug to relieve the building pressure.

Jace's knees fall open and his hips lift off the mattress as I find his prostate and massage it with my finger, coaxing the sensitive nerves to life. "Oh fuck," he gasps. "Fuck, that's good. Give me your cock, now."

I withdraw my fingers and coat my dick with lube, wishing for the first time in my life it wasn't covered in a condom. *Maybe one day, if I find a guy, or girl, who isn't just passing through town.*

Using my hands, I spread Jace wide and press against his opening, sliding back and forth with exaggerated restraint. "Good?"

"Not yet. I need you inside me." He lifts his head up to meet my gaze with a heated look of his own. The desire in his nearly black eyes almost makes me lose control. *Almost.*

I grip the base of my dick and push forward steadily, ready to pull back at the first sign of discomfort. But Jace doesn't resist, wiggling against me as if that could force me deeper. I don't breathe until I'm fully seated, and even then, the pressure surrounding my cock is so mind-blowing it's hard to fill my lungs with air. Then I hear Jace's strained voice. "Move."

Rolling my hips back gently, I slide out, then press forward until I can't go any deeper. Despite the interference of the condom the friction is mind-blowing, Jace's tight ass bearing down all over me. I repeat the motion again and again, driving slow and deep, as Jace pants underneath me, squeezing his cock in his fist to help relieve the ache I'm sure is building there.

"Faster," he whispers as he starts tugging on his junk.

"Let me." I kneel on the bed and push his hand away so I can pump him in rhythm with my thrusts. *Damn he feels good in my fist.*

What begins as slow and steady quickly turns frantic and desperate, both of us too amped up and needy to take our time. A stubborn burn creeps into my stomach and thighs as I drive my cock into Jace, the constant strain on my muscles testing my endurance. But I don't relent. The promise of an orgasm is a powerful motivator.

"Squeeze hard. I like it tight," Jace pants as he gives me control of his pleasure, and something about that sends me spiraling.

"Oh shit," I cry as I pound into him, my fist sliding to the base of his cock each time I bottom out. "I'm close. Tell me you're with me."

The words are barely out of my mouth when tiny contractions kiss the length of my cock, and his dick starts to throb in my fist. Hot, white liquid spurts from the head and trickles down my fingers, the sight of his release triggering my own.

My spine arches as my cock pulses inside him, and pleasure like I've never felt ripples from my core to my limbs. A near feral growl rumbles from my throat, so violently it takes all my focus to stroke him through the finish. *Holy hell – whatever that was, I want more.*

Chapter 4

Jace

"Fuck I needed that." My chest heaves as I try to catch my breath. Sex is always good but getting fucked while someone plays with your junk is next level, and the way Blake worked my dick—I honestly don't think I've ever come so hard.

"My turn next," Blake licks his lips as he withdraws.

There's a hint of anticipation in his tone, like he can't wait to feel me, and for lack of a better term, it makes me giddy. I like that he wants me in every way. That he's already thinking of the next time.

"You haven't bottomed in a while either?" I ask as he tosses the condom in the trash and tosses me a hand towel before coming back to bed, propping his head up with one arm so he can look at me.

His top shoulder lifts just a fraction as I clean off my stomach. "Clients are already laying down on the table, just seems natural for me to top."

"You fuck your clients? Isn't that illegal?" It's hard to keep the surprise out of my voice, though I'm not judging. Blake just doesn't strike me as the type to break the rules. Unnecessary risks, though... That's something I see on a daily basis with filming, so maybe that's all it is.

"I think it's only illegal if people pay for it. Although, it might be a gray area since they're already paying for the massage? But it's not like I'm running a business or anything, I just... you know... Sometimes, massages feel so good that people want more, and I give them what they want." His ears turn a little pink beneath his shaggy hair.

Maybe I'm a dirty fucker, or maybe it's been so long since I had mind blowing sex—with a man or woman—but the idea of going in for or giving a massage that ends with an orgasm is making me sorta hard. *Again.*

I roll to my side so I'm facing him, propping my head on my hand just like his is. "Do you do that with only men or..."

"Women too. Only a handful of people are interested in more than the massage, so I'm not really picky about gender if the chemistry is there. That's why my friend and I started working at the spa actually, although the idea was to meet people you could hook up with later. Somewhere along the line the meeting up later part became an extra step."

Blake's voice fades as he finishes talking, giving me the impression he's embarrassed or ashamed. He doesn't need to feel that way with me, though. Living on the road, I've had my fair share of convenient hookups.

I grab his free hand with mine, stroking my thumb over his, both to reassure him that I don't give a shit about his past and because I just want to touch him. "I can't see you needing to get a job to meet people. You don't exactly fade into the background. I'm sure most women think the same thing I did when I first saw you."

"What was that?" His eyes shoot to mine, a tiny smile pulling at his lip.

I look down at our naked bodies. "Let's just say I got my wish. Seriously though, why get a job to meet people?"

"I'm not sure you noticed, but Katah Vista doesn't have a large female population. Full-timers, anyway. Ryder thought we'd meet girls if we worked in the spa."

"Girls?" I pull my brows together. "He doesn't know you like men, too?"

"No one does." Blake's head shifts back and forth. "In Katah Vista, if one person knows the whole town does, and as far as I know, I'm the only bisexual person there. It's easier to pretend I'm not different than to bring that kind of attention into my life."

"People wouldn't approve?" I glide my thumb over the back of his hand, wondering when the last time was that I held hands with *anyone... Fucking hell, this feels nice.* Blake watches the motion a moment before answering.

"It's more that I'd be the only one with the label, and I didn't want to be singled out like that. Even if it wasn't intentional, people might still do it, like '*You know, Blake, the bi mountain bike coach*' instead of just '*You know, Blake, the mountain bike coach.*' That's why the spa thing is perfect. I get to fulfill that need without the scrutiny."

"So, you meet all your *needs* there?" I shoot him a coy smile as he finally takes his eyes off our hands.

"When you say it like that it sounds shady." A wave of red creeps across his cheeks.

"No more than hooking up with fans we meet on the road, I imagine. I've never had any male fans hit me up, though."

"Does that mean you're in the closet?" He holds his breath, waiting for my answer.

I chew my lip, searching for the best way to answer. "Not exactly. It's not something I keep secret, but it's never come up before so most of the guys have only ever seen me with women. Axel knows, though. You've got me curious about this spa thing." I circle back to what's quickly becoming a new fantasy of mine. "Do you get a lot of men *and* women coming through the spa?"

"Women come in more than men, but only like one in ten girls want the happy ending and three of five guys do."

"How do you know people want the happy ending?"

"Guys are obvious." He shoots me a knowing look that has my cock stirring to life. "With women it's less so, but they'll still give a little moan or angle their hips if they want more. You learn to read the signs."

"So, if I had come in for that massage?" I lift my eyebrows.

"What do you think?" His eyes start to cloud with lust.

"I think I haven't been this turned on in ages."

***

Blake's features are softer when he sleeps. Not that he has a hard look about him, but there's maybe a hint of sadness in his eyes, almost like he's lonely despite having lots of friends around him. I get that.

Traveling with Axel and the rest of our crew, I'm constantly surrounded by people. Yet only one of them really knows me.

Axel and I virtually grew up together—he lived with my family for several years—so he knows all my secrets. And my sexuality isn't a secret per se, at least not in the sense that it's forbidden to talk about. I just don't broadcast it.

There aren't many gay or bi people in the world of motocross, at least not that I've seen, but women are plentiful. It's not hard to find one to share a bed with. If I bumped into a man I wanted to sleep with I wouldn't hesitate, but since that hasn't happened there hasn't been much reason to discuss the fact that I like men, too. And maybe it makes me an asshole, but I don't feel like I should have to. Straight people don't have to explain themselves, so why should I?

Would the guys around me be surprised to learn I like men? Probably. Would they care? I'm honestly not sure. Even if they did, it wouldn't bother me. Most of them come and go with the seasons since the sponsors dictate who goes where, so if anyone did object to my lifestyle it'd be no big deal. Axel is the only constant in my life, more brother than friend, and he doesn't care who I sleep with. He's also careful not to bring up my sexuality unless I do, which means I'm a little like Blake in that most people around me don't know the real me. I do have Axel though, while Blake doesn't seem to have anyone.

That must make him feel especially isolated. No wonder he's comfortable in his little Katah Vista bubble. Even though he's sort of alone inside it, he probably feels less alone there around his friends and neighbors than he does in places where no one knows him at all.

Blake shifts slightly, and the mattress dips under his weight. That's not something I'm used to, but I enjoy it. *I like the solid presence of another man next to me when I wake up.* So does my cock, apparently. And his, if the tented sheet is any indication.

Reaching between my legs, I give myself a slow, firm tug to relieve the pressure. God, what I wouldn't give for another night. But work calls. Axel's competing this weekend, and I need to be there to film his run for the dirt bike movie we're shooting. Even though it's supposed to showcase his trail riding and not the competition circuit, the sponsors want footage to supplement what we recorded on the trails, and that means getting to the track early enough to scout out the best places to shoot. *Damn, I wish we had more time.*

I take my hand off my dick and brush a stray curl off Blake's forehead. *Why is that so satisfying?* He stirs, eyes blinking the room into focus as he stretches his arms above his head, showing off two firm pecs with a smattering of hair dusting the nipples.

"Morning." I trail my finger over his shoulder.

"Morning. What time is it?"

"Eight. What time is your meeting today?"

"Not until ten, but I need to get back to my room and shower."

"You could shower here. Looks like you either need a cold one, or some company." I jerk my head towards the erection he's sporting, and a wave of lust washes over his face.

"Should've woken me up earlier," he groans, fisting himself. "I'm not sure I've got time. When do you have to get on the road?"

"As soon as possible. I need to be at the track before tomorrow and it's almost a ten-hour drive." When I told Blake I had to leave today he was disappointed, but he didn't try to make any plans or promises for a next time. I sort of expected him to since he knows Axel is living in Katah Vista now, which gives me more reason to be there. But I guess he doesn't want anything more than a one-night stand. I'm not even sure I can offer more, anyway.

Now that Axel has made the decision not to travel as much, my future is sort of in limbo, professionally speaking. *My future*. That's not something I've given much thought to before now. I took it for granted, focusing on Axel and hoping he'd ride forever. While he's not retiring yet, it's on the horizon, considering he's already decided not to make the bike movies that usually occupy our time in the off season.

What do I do when he retires completely? Do I hitch myself to another rider to film? Do I go to a network, filming entire competitions as opposed to individual riders? Do I leave motocross altogether and try to get a foothold somewhere else, like TV?

I'm fortunate in that I've made a lot of money and spent very little of it living on the road, but that doesn't mean I can sit on my ass the rest of my life. And if I'm not working with Axel, my ass has no reason parking itself in Katah Vista. It's not exactly a hotbed of activity for motocross. Or cameramen.

No, my future probably doesn't lie in the valley, which means not making any plans is the smart move. That doesn't mean I want Blake to leave without a proper goodbye.

I leap out of bed and hold out my hand. "Since we're both in a rush, we better make this quick."

"Make what quick?" He studies my hand a second before taking it.

"Getting each other clean." I pull him up and lead him to the bathroom, where I make sure we're both spotless, after we get dirty of course.

Chapter 5

Blake

My last moments with Jace run through my mind on a constant loop as I get dressed, making it hard to concentrate.

"How does this work?"

"How does what work?" He pauses at the door, tilting his head to the side as he studies me.

"The morning after goodbye. It's not really a thing when you're just having a quickie at the spa." My neck heats up as the words leave my mouth.

Jace's eyes grow wide. "You think I'm any better at this? I usually pretend to be passed out."

"You sound even more shallow than me." I can't stop the laugh bubbling up from my chest, which expands fully, knowing I'm not the only one who tries to avoid these awkward situations. Strangely, this moment doesn't feel awkward. Just unfinished. *That doesn't feel like something I should admit, though.*

"I guess I'm better at sex than being a gentleman or whatever." He rubs a hand over the back of his neck.

"Hey, at least you brought me back to your room. I don't usually make it past the massage table. Or get the other person's name." I blow out a

frustrated breath, wondering if my attempt to lighten the mood went too far. Fortunately, he doesn't seem offended.

"Don't give me too much credit. I still kept you up most of the night knowing, full well, you have a big meeting today." He presses his lips together, eyes traveling over my body.

"And you've got a big drive." My expression mirrors his.

"One more for the road." Jace's strong hand wraps around my neck and pulls me forward, crushing my lips to his in a bruising, breathless kiss. "Now get out of here before you make us both late." He gives me a sexy little wink as he opens the door, and I steal one last kiss before I dart into the hall.

As far as goodbyes go, I think it went okay. If only I could kick this, *I wish it didn't have to end,* feeling. I didn't say anything about it—neither did Jace—but in my gut I know we were both thinking that. We also both seemed to sense that saying something out loud might ruin it.

Call it years of living with a secret, but for my part, asking to see him again when I'm not out didn't seem fair. Even though he's not shouting from the rooftops that he's bi, Jace doesn't appear to be hiding the truth the way I am. Asking to see him again when I can't promise if or when I'll come out seems selfish. Although, I might've spoken up if his best friend hadn't just moved to Katah Vista. I figure with Axel living a few minutes away from me there's a decent chance I'll cross paths with Jace again, so I figured I'd play it cool instead of trying to force something. I'm letting my future unfold however it wants.

It's hard to explain, but something about being born this way left me with the sense I'm not fully in control. After all, being bi isn't exactly an easy life, so I wouldn't have chosen it. I guess that's why I always believed that when I find *the one*—man or woman—I'm meant to spend my life with, then their gender will determine what I tell people about my sexuality. After all, if *the one* turns out to be a woman then there's no point in saying anything. If it's a man, I'll come out as gay. Either way, I've always assumed that I'll identify as one or the other when the time comes, and the person I fall in love with will dictate how I ultimately choose to live my life. Some people might call it believing in fate, and to a certain extent I think that's true, although it's just as much about practicality. Letting circumstance determine the outcome.

I'm not saying it'll make Jace *the one* if we run into each other again, though at that point, I'm going to take it as a sign worth paying attention to, especially after the night we just shared. And I'm not just referring to the part between the sheets. Yes, the sex was *phenomenal*—hands down the best I've ever had with a man—and yeah, that's a huge part of what's making it so hard for me to concentrate on getting ready. But what's really got my mind spinning is that all the time before and in between sex was just as incredible.

Jace and I have lots of the same interests, from bikes to movies to the type of women we like (sporty yet feminine). He's more worldly than I am, having traveled all over to film Axel's videos and attend his events, and as a result he's got a huge network of friends all around the world. But he never made me feel inferior about that. Actually, he seemed intrigued by my whole small-town existence, even though it plays a role in keeping me in the closet.

It didn't feel like he was judging me for wanting to stay put, or for using my job as a way to explore and satisfy my needs. It was a huge relief, considering he isn't actively keeping secrets the way I am. I appreciate the fact he didn't challenge my reasons or press me to change my habits. He just accepted me at face value.

All in all, I felt comfortable with Jace in a way I haven't experienced with anyone else before. I guess that's why, if I ever decide to date a man, I could see it being him. And why I'm sort of hoping this morning isn't the last time I see him. But I've never tried to force anything with someone I had an interest in, and I'm not going to start now. Whatever happens, happens. In the meantime, I'll just take each day as it comes, the way I always have.

***

"Jackson." A tall, wiry man with unruly blonde hair holds up his fist.

"Blake." I bump my knuckles against his. "Thanks for taking the time to meet with me."

"Of course. I never turn down an opportunity to show off our bike park. Have you ridden it, yet?"

"I got in too late yesterday." I shake my head sheepishly. *Nice job dumbass. How are you supposed to talk bike park details if you don't know what they are?*

"Well, this won't take all day. I'll give you a lift ticket so you can check it out when we're done. Maybe I'll even take a few runs with you. You know... to show you the key details it takes to make an epic park." He grins widely as he holds open the door to his office, and I step inside to what's basically a shrine to biking.

Sketches of some of the first mountain bikes line the walls, showcasing the progression of the technology from those early models to what we use today. There are a few signed jerseys, framed along with action pictures of the rider on the track, hanging on either side of the door, where Jackson can see them from his desk if he's facing the room.

All he has to do is spin his chair for a clear view of the mountain, and the bikes careening down it.

I'm not an office guy, mainly because the ones I've seen make me think of a prison cell, but this one doesn't give me claustrophobia. It actually seems pretty comfortable, although with a view like that I wonder how the guy gets any work done. I'd be too tempted to hit the trail. Then again, maybe that's the job, in which case this guy is who I want to be when I grow up.

Taking a seat in the chair across from him so I have a view of the desk, Jackson shows me some of the drawings used to obtain the permits they needed to build the park. Elevation changes are listed along the trail so things like runoff and erosion can be factored into any paths they carve or features they add. It's similar to what I've seen doing trail maintenance, and yet so much more.

Back country trails follow the slope of the mountain while those at the resort sometimes go against it. Of course, all trails work their way down hill, but in the back country we just try to enhance the natural terrain, whereas at the resort they re-engineer it. In some places they've carved giant switchbacks into the side of the hill, effectively turning the trail into a luge. Bridges string gaps together that would otherwise be unrideable, and in some cases, they create a launch point to jump downhill over sections that are too rocky to navigate on a bike. It's a literal playground for adults and it makes me sort of giddy.

I've seen stuff like this before, mostly on YouTube, and I've even ridden a small-scale version of what Jackson's built here when I did my stint in California. But until today, I've never had a before and after glimpse of the trail. The final product is epic, which makes me realize I have zero idea how to build something like this myself.

My stomach sinks as reality sets in, and my breathing becomes labored. Though I suspected as much, some part of me was hoping my experience was enough to land the job of building a park in Katah Vista. That in sending me here, Carter was actually giving me a shot at a job I'm passionate about, one I could turn into a career. And maybe that was his intent. But plans are underway to make the skiable terrain in Katah Vista a world-renowned destination, so it stands to reason Carter will want the same for the bike park, and I'm not that guy. Not if this is the final product he wants.

"Does this help answer your questions about building a park?" Jackson says after finishing his overview of their process.

I offer a wary smile as I run a hand through my hair. "Not even close."

He barks out a laugh. "I get it. A project like this has a way of raising more questions the deeper you dive into it."

"Exactly." I blow out a frustrated breath. "I don't suppose you're available to hire?" We both know that's an offhand suggestion, though truth be told I'm not kidding. I have a feeling Carter wouldn't object to tapping into Jackson's expertise.

He gives me a headshake, wearing a proud grin as he does it. "Sorry. My setup here is too sweet to give up, although my assistant might be game."

"I'll mention that to Carter. Thanks again for your time." I rise and offer him my fist just as he did when we first met. We bump knuckles, though he holds up a finger to keep me from leaving.

"Lift ticket." He thrusts a card into my hand. "Show this to the guys at the counter and they'll get you a day pass."

"I'd love to, but I don't have my bike with me." I feel the heat creeping up my neck. *Could I have been more unprepared for this day?*

"Not a problem. You can try a demo bike." He hands me another card. "That'll get you a free rental. I'm partial to Yeti, but Santa Cruz makes a great bike too, and we've got both in the shop. Take one out for a few runs. I'll try to join you after I finish payroll."

I accept the second card with a nod and head over to the bike shop to gear up, figuring it might make sense to report back on how the park rides. And, okay, I figure I might as well enjoy this perk while I can since it's unlikely I'll be involved in whatever Carter does going forward.

Lift operators load my bike onto the chair for me, and then it's a peaceful ten-minute ride to the top of the hill before another set of attendants have my bike waiting for me when I get off. *I always preach that you have to earn the downhill, but I could seriously get used to having a motor do all the work.*

Choosing a blue for my first run—a warm up—I pedal down a gradual slope before dropping into a series of S curves with berms so high I can lay the bike parallel to the ground as I whip around the turns. *Damn, that's a rush.* Then I'm in the trees, floating over a series of rollers that make my belly drop like I'm on a roller coaster. The run finishes in a meadow with sweeping turns where I can pick up speed despite the fact that I'm barely going downhill.

I hit a black run next, balancing on my pedals as I roll over a rocky steep that mimics a staircase. Then it's onto a dirt section in the trees where roots jut out of the ground to interrupt the smooth flow of the trail. Massive tabletop jumps complete the run, giving me a chance to grab some big air.

By the time I've explored just about every run available, my legs are burning and my chest doesn't feel so hollow. A good bike ride has that effect, wearing me out even as it rejuvenates me. Feeling content, I return the gear and head back to the hotel, intending to shower and order room service. But the quiet of my room feels oppressive after sharing a room with Jace, so I head back to the bar hoping it will distract me for the few hours I have to kill before crawling into bed.

Chapter 6

Becca

The sun has started its descent by the time I catch up enough to call it a day, making me wonder why I bother with vacation when all the stress it's supposed to relieve comes back the moment I see all the work that piled up in my absence. The only consolation is that my to-do list is on the mountain instead of some stuffy office. Jackson may get the bigger paycheck, but I've got the better job, or so I like to believe.

Tossing my bag in the passenger seat, I go through the motions of heading home, only to realize I have nothing to go home to. The fridge is just as bare as the house itself, and I don't have the energy to survive a trip to the grocery store. Even if there was food, it's hard to muster the excitement to cook for one, which is why I've rarely done it since Brian moved out nearly a year ago. Looks like I'm eating out again.

"Hey, Becca. The usual?" Jason sets my favorite beer in front of me, a Hefeweizen with an orange slice.

"I feel like I should say no and try something different, but how do I pass up perfection?" I lift the pint glass to my lips and take a sip, closing my eyes as the cool liquid hits my tongue. *Why does a cold beer taste so good at the end of the day?*

"One Reuben, coming up." He gives me a playful wink as he keys in my order. "How was your trip?"

"Meh. Don't get me wrong, it was nice to see my sister and my nephews, but do you know how exhausting little kids are?"

"How old are they?" he asks as he fills a glass from the tap.

"Charlie is four and Henry is two, and aside from naptime they don't sit still."

"Too young to ride bikes, then?" He arches a knowing brow in my direction, daring me to admit I didn't try to stick them on two wheels.

"Yes, smartass, we did ride bikes. And played superheroes. And watched shows about superheroes. And dressed like them."

"At least you didn't have to play tea party, although I bet the pink hair would've worked well with a princess costume." He gives a long strand a playful tug.

"Take that back. This isn't princess pink, it's flamingo." I snatch my hair and yank it out of his grip.

"Why flamingo?" he frowns.

"Cause those birds are tough as hell," I recite my favorite fact. In addition to being aggressive when the situation calls for it, flamingos can withstand some pretty cold temperatures, so while they look gentle, they can be fierce. I like to think I'm the same way. They're also exceptionally loyal, which is maybe why I stayed with Brian longer than I should've, but that's beside the point.

Jason laughs and drifts off to help another customer, leaving me to sit with my thoughts, which aren't the best company. I've been feeling sort of off lately—hence my vacation—although it didn't have the effect I wanted.

Despite having a job I love, I feel stuck in a rut. Professionally I've hit the ceiling, until Jackson retires, anyway. Which likely won't happen anytime soon given that he's only about five years older than me. Personally, I'm a disaster, still bitter about my last relationship and questioning myself at every turn thanks to Brian's insinuation that he cheated because I'm "not feminine enough."

Right after he dropped that bombshell I decided to retaliate with a little affair of my own, and for a moment there I managed to convince myself that I was plenty feminine. My partner certainly thought so, and even though it was just the one night he made me feel better about myself than Brian ever did, despite two years together. That night got me through months of self-doubt, but here I am, still single and unintentionally celibate nearly a year later, which is starting to freak me out.

Part of that is my fault. I'm not good at putting myself out there, and I can't really expect people to approach me if I don't look approachable. But—and here's the rub—maybe guys don't want a woman who wears bike shorts and sports bras instead of dresses and sexy lingerie, just like Brian said.

No matter how much I try to ignore it, the guy is in my head, and I'm starting to wonder if the only way to get him out is a change of scenery. That's the real reason I went to visit my sister, to see if a fresh start might get me out of my funk. Only her scenery didn't do anything for me. I want green mountains, not red cliffs, so for now I guess I'm home?

I take another sip of beer as my eyes wander around the restaurant, landing on a stranger sitting at the opposite end of the bar. *Talk about new scenery.* Although, he's not exactly a stranger in the sense that I recognize him from the mountain.

Some people just belong on two wheels, and this guy is one of them. He rides like the bike is an extension of his body, tethering him to the trail despite the fact that he's not actually touching it. Fast but not reckless, he whipped over terrain a novice would consider a joyride, and floated over obstacles even seasoned riders don't attempt. I'll own it—the way he rides made me wet with desire—and that's saying something because I'm hard to impress. I couldn't take my eyes off him, strictly because of his grace on the bike, and once I got a look at that face I was done for.

Strong jaw with just a hint of stubble. Eyes that studied the trail with a mix of determination and wonder. The hint of a smile when he got to the bottom of the mountain, almost like he was at peace and trying to stay in the moment. I know because that's exactly how I feel on my bike.

His effortless skill mesmerized me, to the point that I almost, *almost*, built up the courage to approach him. But I lost my nerve when Brian's current girlfriend sashayed past on her way to her shift at the bar. One look at the slender thighs poking out from her short skirt and my stomach sank, knowing the calves beneath my knee-length shorts were no comparison. So, I watched him ride off, a strange pang of regret rippling through my chest over the loss of something I'd never have.

And now he's here, right across the bar and... *Shit*. He caught me staring.

I lift my glass, an awkward little "*cheers*", as if that will somehow make it any less embarrassing to get caught mid-ogle. Instead of lifting his glass in return he spins to his right, then his left, looking behind him.

Oh. My. God. Gorgeous *and* modest? That's unexpected. And sort of awesome. I stifle a giggle when he realizes there's no one around him and gives me an almost bashful smile. My chest constricts with that strange little yearning thing again. Although now, instead of a dull ache it's an acute pain, like someone pricked me with a fucking needle.

Suddenly the idea of watching him walk away is more painful than the idea of talking to him. *Man up, Becca.*

Tossing back the last of my liquid courage, I make my way around to his side of the bar, grateful that he's focused on something in his hand rather than me as I approach.

"Hi. Um, can I sit?" I point to the empty stool next to him.

His brows disappear beneath his hair before he moves to pull out the stool. "Yeah. Please."

"Becca." I give him my hand.

"Blake." Sparks travel up my arm the second his warm fingers wrap around mine. *I haven't felt electricity like that since... Stop it. Now is not the time to think of the rebound guy.*

We linger there a second, staring at each other with our hands clasped, until he clears his throat and darts his gaze to the barstool. I let my hand slip away from his and take a seat.

"Enjoying your visit?" I press my lips between my teeth as soon as the words are out. *That's the best you can do?*

"What makes you think I'm just visiting?" He cocks his head to the side.

"The hotel key card you're spinning on the bar." I nod toward the hand resting on the counter, and he visibly starts. It's cute. "Doing some heavy thinking?"

"Um, just the usual for a guy sitting alone at a bar." He casts me a sideways glance as he sips his beer.

"And that is?"

"What the fuck am I doing alone at a bar?" His shoulders seem to slump a bit as he gives me a guilty smile.

I bite my lip to stop the grin tugging at it. "At least you have the excuse of visiting. I, on the other hand, sit at this bar alone quite frequently."

"I find that hard to believe."

"It's true. I think I might put off a *'stay back'* vibe."

"Why's that?" His tone is purely curious. I like that.

"I'm not very good at small talk."

"You're doing fine so far. Although, now I'm wondering why you came over, if you don't like talking."

"I'm not sure I would've if you didn't catch me staring. But I figured since I missed you on the mountain, I should at least talk to you now."

"You saw me on the mountain?" Those brows lift into his hair again.

Swallowing my nerves, I nod. "I like the way you ride."

"You bike?" His eyes seem to light up.

"A little." I lift my shoulder just a fraction, hoping he won't push for details. Thanks to Brian, I tend to believe guys only pretend to approve of a woman working in the industry, and I'd rather not ruin what could be a fun night by learning whether Blake fits that pattern. Fortunately, Jason heads that off by setting food in front of us.

"Two Reubens, and a side of Ranch for your fries." He winks at me. "Get you another round?"

Blake and I both nod and Jason goes to refill the drinks.

"I guess I made a good choice?" Blake darts his gaze toward our plates.

"The best, but you really should swap the Ketchup for Ranch."

His nose crinkles as he watches me pop a Ranch-dipped fry in my mouth, though when I raise my brows in challenge, he grabs a fry and helps himself to my dressing. Tilting his head to the side he blinks his hazel eyes as he chews, almost like he's letting the flavor coat every inch of his tongue. Then he swallows and slowly meets my gaze. "Not bad."

"You thought I'd steer you wrong?" My jaw falls open in mock offense.

"Well, you do have pink hair." The corner of his lip pulls upward like he's fighting a smile.

"That's because blonde, like Ketchup, is boring. And I'm not boring." I have no idea where that retort came from, but it's actually true. I'll claim insecure, awkward, and tomboyish, but not boring. Although, considering I order the same thing every time I eat here, maybe I just don't want to admit the truth.

"We're basing personality on hair color? Okay, what does mine say about me?" He takes a bite of his sandwich and chews with a sly grin, like he's daring me to answer. *Alright, I like puzzles.*

"Well, the light brown says you blend in, but the shaggy length and hint of curl at the tip says you're not a rule follower, so I'm going to go with paradox. You're familiar and not at the same time."

Blake's hand freezes halfway to his mouth, jaw hanging open. Then he clears his throat and looks at his plate. "That's deep."

"Am I right?" I nudge his arm with my elbow.

"I'd say the length means I'm lazy." He reaches for his beer, washing down his sandwich. "But yeah, I guess I blend in."

I cock my head and study him. "No. You don't blend. Not the way you ride a bike."

"Now you're just trying to make me feel like I'm not average." He nudges me back.

"I did tell you I'm not good at small talk." I bite my lip to stop myself from saying anything else awkward.

"This isn't small talk, it's conversation. I like it." There's a raw honesty to his voice that makes me believe him, even though I think my personality assessment rattled him.

"What makes this a conversation?" My voice is oddly soft, almost like I'm afraid of the answer. *Maybe I am.*

"Conversation makes you think."

"Small talk doesn't?" I know I sound skeptical, but how do you start talking to someone if you don't first think about what to say?

He swallows even though there's nothing in his mouth. "If I asked what's your favorite sandwich, do you have to think about that or can you answer right away?"

"Rueben," I say on autopilot.

"And if I asked why pink is any less boring than say, red? Or purple?"

I hold my breath in my lungs, replaying his words. "I'd say pink is unpredictable. It can be quiet and soft, or loud and bold."

Blake's eyes meet mine, something like pride and *desire* in his gaze. "See what I mean?"

Wow. A flood of thoughts and emotions race through my brain faster than I can register what they are. He's got my head and my heart working in overdrive, both of which seem to be screaming at me not to let this moment end. I mean, it will eventually since he's just visiting, but until then? I don't think I could walk away from him right now if I tried.

"Do you want to get out of here?" I whisper.

"My hotel is around the corner."

***

"You win. Pink is not boring." Blake stumbles toward the bathroom to discard the condom, coming back to bed with an almost dazed look on his face.

"Are you saying hair color dictates how good a person is in bed?" I pinch his hip, a *tiny* warning to think about his answer.

He squirms out of my reach. "I'm saying I've tried that position before and it was hot seeing the way your back arched while you rode me. It was even hotter to feel your hand playing with my balls. *You're* the one correlating hair color with good sex. Although, based on recent experience, I agree with you. Pink hair equals good in bed."

"That's so not what I was saying." I roll my eyes dramatically. "But I'll let it pass since you're giving me a compliment. I think."

"Of course it's a compliment." He rolls to his side to face me. "You don't take those very well, do you?"

I didn't realize I'd given off that impression, but since he's not wrong I won't argue. That doesn't mean I'll spill all my baggage about the challenges I face as a woman in the industry.

Rolling my head to face him I offer a weak smile. "Most of the time they come with a qualifier, at least in my experience. You ride well *for a girl*. You're smart *for a girl*. Stuff like that. Or they're about something arbitrary, like how you look, and that's more of a genetic outcome than something I actually did, you know?"

"So I shouldn't say you're good in bed *for a girl*?" The corner of his lip pulls up as he tries not to laugh, though the laughter doesn't quite reach his eyes. I wonder why.

I wrap my hand around his cock–*how is it still sorta hard*–and tighten my grip with a wicked smirk. "Say *for a girl* again. I dare you."

"Is this supposed to be a threat?" He arches a brow in that sexy way only guys can pull off.

"You think I won't squeeze?"

"I hope you do. Maybe this time I can be on top. I'd like to watch you come next."

That's so unexpected I let go. "You want to...watch?"

"You say that like it's weird." A tiny line forms between his brows.

"Not weird just...not something I'm used to." I trap my lips between my teeth, wishing I could take the words back.

Blake rubs a finger over the bridge of his nose. "I'm gonna need more information than that. Has no one ever watched you come before?"

"I...well...once or twice maybe." I think back to the rebound guy, who wouldn't let us cover our encounter in darkness. Then Brian, who always insisted on it. I'm not intending to mention either of those things until I realize Blake is still staring at me intently. "It's not something you see very well in the dark."

"I'm guessing since the lights are on now it wasn't you who insisted on the dark?"

I shake my head no.

"Why did *he*?" Blake doesn't clarify who *he* is, though I get the sense he can guess it's someone who used to be important to me.

"If I had to guess, he could pretend I was someone else in the dark." *Shit*. I didn't mean to say that, either. *Why do my words just spill out in front of him?*

Blake brushes a pink strand away from my face. "I can't pretend to know what that would be like–I've never really dated anyone so I don't have that kind of scar–but I do know you shouldn't let this one become permanent."

I try to swallow the lump in my throat before it turns into a full-on sob–pretty sure crying is frowned upon during a one-night stand–although that's no easy feat considering it's the nicest thing anyone has said to me. Ever.

"I'll try not to," I whisper.

"Good." He plants a soft kiss on my lips. "Now lay back and let me between those legs. I'd love nothing more than to see those pretty blue eyes staring at mine when I take you over the edge."

Slowly, gently, he does.

Chapter 7

Blake

One minute, I'm nursing a beer, wishing Jace had been able to stay for another night. The next, a striking woman with bubble gum pink hair is at my side, and for the second morning in a row, I'm not alone when I wake up.

I'd like to claim that's because I was feeling lonely without Jace's company, but the truth is I was just as drawn to her as I had been him, and I'm not sure how to feel about that.

Up until last night, I was half convinced Jace would play a role in my future. The way we clicked—in bed and out—I've never experienced that before. The only reason I didn't latch onto it and try to force another encounter is because in my gut I feel like that's bound to happen with his best friend living in my hometown. Then I met Becca, and it was a lightning strike all over again. I didn't want to admit it at first because it felt like that would be betraying Jace, even though you can't betray someone you aren't technically with. But the pull toward Becca was just as strong.

She's a brave little thing under that soft outer shell. It's clear she's been hurt before, which makes me want to wrap her in my arms and shield her from the world. She doesn't need that, though. She can hold her own, in conversation and in bed, where she's both ravenous and adventurous.

We got back to my room and straight up devoured each other, fucking against the wall because we were too turned on to make it to the bed. The next round was less frenzied, both of us exploring and savoring the way we moved together. And in between we talked with ease.

By some unspoken agreement, we didn't delve into personal details. It's almost as if we purposely danced around them, knowing it'd make saying goodbye harder. But we talked about places we want to travel to, scars we discovered on our bodies, and her strange fascination with flamingos. Becca also confessed to being scarred by a former relationship, and I admitted to never being in one before, which led to what I can only describe as making love.

I'm not entirely sure that's what it was, given I've never done anything besides fuck, but the gentle glide of our bodies, the way her legs cradled me and held me tight, our faces hovering so close we shared each other's air as we came... It sounds cheesy as hell, but I swear I felt that orgasm in my chest, and not in a *'catch your breath after a workout'* kind of way but in a *'did you feel that too'* kind of way.

Now I'm lying here, Becca curled in my arms, and it feels just as right as waking up next to Jace did. How is that even possible? Throughout my entire life I've believed things would unfold the way they're meant to, and in the span of two days I meet two different people I feel instantly connected to. Why is the universe fucking with me?

The only reason I'm not totally losing my shit right now is because neither Jace nor Becca live in Katah Vista. It's the only thing keeping me out of some taboo love triangle. Then there's the fact, for all I know, the connections I feel are one-sided. Or I'm feeling them more deeply than they are. Either way, I'm sort of reeling over these two people who are each making me yearn for more.

My watch vibrates on my wrist, signaling it's time for me to get up so I can make my flight. I reach over Becca to silence it, and movement makes her stir, nuzzling her face against my chest. *Damn, that feels nice.*

"Morning." I kiss the top of her head.

"Morning." Lithe arms reach above her head as she stretches, the sheet drifting lower until the tops of her perky breasts are exposed. It takes all my willpower not to cup one in my hand. My fingers ache to squeeze the plump mound and bring her nipple to a beaded point the way I now know she loves. "What time is it?"

"Seven." I run a finger along her arm as she drops them back to her side. *So smooth.* "I'd ask you to go to breakfast, but I have to get to the airport."

"Do you have time for a shower?" She twists toward me to run her fingers over my chest.

"If I knew that was on the table, I'd have woken you up earlier." I twirl a strand of hair around my fingers. *I love the feel of long hair, and I especially loved pulling on it last night.* "I can't miss my flight, though."

Becca places a soft kiss to my pec before rolling away to get dressed. A part of me is relieved I'm still in bed because that sweet little gesture would've made my knees buckle.

As she's dressing, I pull on my boxers so I can walk her to the door, and by the time they're on, she's wearing those cute bike shorts that highlight her sleek calves. *Feminine and sporty – I love that combination.* I hold out my hand and she takes it, allowing me to pull her against my body.

"I've only done the morning-after goodbye thing once, so I sort of suck at it." I brush her hair behind her ear and place a gentle kiss on her lips.

"You're doing fine so far." She borrows my words from last night, looking up at me with a smile I know is forced.

Damn... I wish I knew what to do here. I don't have the same gut feeling about seeing her again that I did with Jace, which makes me tempted to do something to change it. That would hardly be fair to her when I have no intention of leaving Katah Vista. That leaves me in the same place I was yesterday morning, at the mercy of whatever fate or the universe have in store.

"I'm sure it sounds cheesy, but I really do hope I'll see you again one day." Despite being totally lame, that feels like the only safe thing to say.

"I hope so, too." She rises up on her toes to give me one last kiss. "Bye, Blake."

"Bye." I hold the door open so she can walk out, closing it before I'm tempted to see if she looks back. Then I get dressed and throw my shit in my bag, trying not to acknowledge that I'm suddenly reluctant to go home.

***

I don't even drop my bags at home. Instead, I beeline for Murphy's, my favorite restaurant, to grab a bite to eat and distract myself from the thoughts running through my head.

I'm no stranger to casual hookups, but I've never had one—let alone two—that stuck with me after it was over. More importantly, can I even classify what happened with Jace and Becca as casual? I might've had just one night with each of them, but those nights felt meaningful. I mean, pillow talk, cuddling, goodbye kisses—those are the kinds of things you do when the other person is important to you, I think. Could either of them be important after only one night? Could they both be? My brain wants to say no; there's no logic to that train of thought. My gut is still undecided. Why else would I still be thinking of two people I can't have?

Lost in my head my feet take me halfway to my favorite barstool before I register my name being called. Turning toward the sound, I find Axel, Deacon, Cade, Ryder and Carter sitting at a corner table.

"How was the trip?" Cade offers me a fist bump. I shoot Carter a confused glance as I press my knuckles against Cade's.

"I told the guys I sent you to Utah to check out a bike park," Carter confirms. *Wow he's got twelve percent of a plan and he's sharing it with everyone? He's come a long way from the days where he kept all his ideas to himself.*

Pulling up a chair I sit at the head of the table and answer Cade. "It was great, actually. The bike park is amazing."

"That's one of Jace's favorite downhill parks." Axel reaches for a fry from a basket they're all sharing. "Did you see him there? He said he was gonna hit the mountain a few days before meeting me at the next competition."

"I did, actually. We grabbed a beer." I turn to flag down a server before my expression can give anything away. Even though Axel knows about Jace, I'm not sure that means it's okay to say anything beyond what I just did. And I definitely don't need the rest of the guys to notice anything weird.

"Well, what did you learn?" Carter prompts after I place my order.

"We may have the basic infrastructure to get bikes up the mountain, but that's about all we have." I scratch my head, which is suddenly itchy with everyone watching me. Well, everyone but Ryder, who's leaning his head against the wall with a distant look on his face. *Maybe talking about bikes will get through to him. He loves riding as much as the rest of us.*

"The right way to do this is to build trails with varying degrees of difficulty, just like the ski runs. Green would be nice and flowy without anything like rocks or tree roots on the trail, black would have lots of technical elements and jumps, and blue would fall somewhere in the middle. Anything we build would have to factor in snow runoff and erosion, and carving the trail won't be as simple as digging with a few shovels. Depending on the features we add we'd need some heavy equipment."

"Okay." Carter doesn't seem phased.

Deacon claps his hand together and rubs them like he's plotting something big. "I love working with big machinery."

My eyes dart between him and Carter. "I thought you were a landscaper?"

"He and Cade both have the commercial license needed to run the equipment, but they'll be following the plans you give them."

"Me?" I point at my chest. "I'm not really qualified to build something on the scale we're talking about."

"What about Jackson?" Axel suggests. "You saw what he did in Utah, ask him to do it here."

"I sorta did that already." I shoot a nervous glance toward Carter. "Not that I offered him a job or anything, I just floated the idea of him coming here as kind of a joke and he said he has it pretty good where he is. He did mention something about an assistant though."

"Bec." Axel grins. "I've heard the name before. If you can't get Jackson, then Bec's the next best thing. They both put a lot of time into that park, and you'd be lucky to get either one. Which run was your favorite?" he asks me.

The rest of the table hangs on our every word as Axel and I talk about the different trails, all of them practically salivating at the idea of having so many downhill options a chairlift away. For a moment, I get lost in the conversation, reliving how it felt to soar over the trail as it wove through the trees. Then this 'Bec' creeps into my mind, and I wonder whether his presence will mean there isn't any room for me on this project.

"Did Jackson say how long it took to build the park?" Carter asks after Axel and I run out of trails to rave about.

"He didn't. Although, I got the impression between the planning and building it was a few years."

"I guess we better get started then. I'm going to see if I can convince this Bec to give us a hand. Assuming I'm successful, I'll need you to be in charge of gathering whatever resources are needed." Carter's gaze falls on me.

"Me?" I point to myself for the second time in an hour.

"Of course, you. You know biking and you know everyone in town. Things will move a lot faster if you're Bec's contact for things like equipment and personnel. And my guess is that'll be a full-time position, so you may want to give your notice at the spa."

I feel my jaw moving though no words come out. *Did he just offer me a job?*

"Unless you want to keep working there?" Carter watches me with a confused look, apparently mistaking my silence for hesitation instead of shock.

"*No!* Nope. I can give my two weeks," I stutter.

"Good. Stop by my office tomorrow and we'll talk salary. I'm thinking..."

Carter trails off as Ryder slumps forward, head landing on the table with a thud. *Shit.* I'm embarrassed to say in all the excitement about the resort I wasn't paying attention to what he was doing. "Should I be worried about this?" Carter looks around the table for input.

"I'm not sure," Cade scrubs a hand down his face.

"It's only been a month since he lost his brother," I explain, not because Carter isn't aware, he just doesn't know Ryder all that well since he joined our group of friends right about the time Ryder's brother passed.

"A month isn't that long." Deacon scratches his jaw. "And he isn't really hurting anybody by drinking his feelings."

"He could be hurting his career if he isn't ready to ride when the snowboard season starts," Carter points out.

"Maybe we cut him some slack until then?" Deacon shrugs. I'm not sure I agree, but that's probably not my place anymore.

Though he's still one of my closest friends, Ryder and I drifted apart after he turned pro. He was always on the road and I was always here, and while he was gone I pulled back from the whole 'pick up as many tourists as you can' game that we played when we were younger. Deacon slid into the void I left, and the two of them are like wingmen, now. That doesn't bother me, except in moments like this when I wonder if Deacon's making the right call. Then again, I've never lost someone so close to me. Maybe a month or two of drowning your sorrows is acceptable.

"We should keep a closer eye on him, though," Cade elbows his cousin.

"Yeah, probably," Deacon agrees. "Anyone want to help me get him home?"

"I'm in." I toss a few bills on the table as I stand up.

"I've got this." Carter tosses my money back at me. "It was sort of a work meeting, anyway."

"Okay, thanks." I make plans to stop by his office the next day, then help Deacon cart Ryder home, feeling somewhat ashamed that it took Ryder's pain to make me stop thinking about the dilemmas in my own life.

Chapter 8

Jace

"You've lived there what, two weeks, and you want me to move to Katah Vista?" Axel's been in my car all of thirty seconds, and in the same breath as he thanked me for picking him up from the airport he sprung this bombshell on me.

"Two and a half. And I was working on this plan before I moved there, I just didn't want to say anything until I had it mostly worked out."

I shoot him a sideways glance as I merge onto the highway and toward the arena where we'll spend the next few days. "You couldn't have waited until after the competition to say something? I mean, I've only had a few weeks to digest the fact that this coming off season is gonna look real different than it usually does, and now you want me to relocate?"

Using my middle finger, I scratch the side of my head, not so subtly flicking him off. His answering snort tells me he knows I'm giving him shit, even though he's legit throwing me for a loop.

"Yeah, when you put it that way it sounds like I'm jerking you around, but I promise I'm not." He runs a hand through the disheveled blond hair that made him a favorite among the female fans.

"I know switching up the schedule so I could spend more time with Lennon puts you out of a job for part of the year, so I've made a plan to fill that time."

"A plan that requires me to move to Katah Vista? I know you're attached to me, but Lennon might think three's a crowd." I'm being sort of a prick, but I really did intend to give Axel the space to be with his girl by doing my own thing in the off season. And—after my encounter in Utah—I'm a little worried about how a move would be interpreted by the guy involved in said encounter.

Blake and I left things undefined, and since he's the only one of us with a permanent address that he didn't ask me to visit, I can't help wondering if that's because he wanted to limit things to a night. Even though I'm certain we both felt something more than a hookup, he's still completely in the closet, and he might not be ready to leave it. That would explain the lack of an invitation to swing by if I were ever in town to see Axel.

"Lennon's totally on board with my plan and with you moving there," Axel brings my mind back to the present. "I think she thinks it's a good way to keep me from being underfoot at Murphy's."

This time it's me who snorts. Lennon is the biggest workaholic I know—she nearly chose her restaurant over Axel—and I have no doubt she'll support any plan that might keep him too busy to bother her.

"Alright, so what is this grand plan?"

Axel spends the next twenty minutes telling me about this horse barn he wants to turn into an indoor training facility. A place where kids can learn how to do the dirt bike tricks that have made him famous. Apparently, there's enough space to ride *and* set up a foam pit to practice jumps without having to land them. Not to mention a bunk room of sorts where people could stay if they don't live in the area.

I never figured myself for an instructor, but I know enough to teach people how to throw tricks. After all, I used to do it myself, which is how I first met Axel as a little kid. The two of us trained together for years until I got more interested in filming than riding. In theory, that would make coaching a job to consider, and for the most part it doesn't sound like a bad gig, since it would mean working with my best friend in an industry I love. It's the location that has me concerned.

If I'm in Katah Vista, I know I'll want to see Blake. Putting aside the fact that we had some of the best sex I've had in a while, I like the guy. It was fun to talk about biking without focusing on the technical aspects, like where to set up the camera for the best shot. And I like how Blake listened intently when I talked about some of the places I've been. The morning after, I was disappointed that I couldn't swing another night with him. It's a feeling I don't get often, so the idea of seeing him again—*regularly*—has a lot of appeal.

I've never had a regular thing before, and I get the impression he hasn't either. It doesn't sound like the worst idea, if every night would be like the one we had together. Maybe we could try the dating thing? After all, it's working pretty well for Axel, which makes me think I might enjoy having a person of my own. A boyfriend. But I have no idea whether Blake would want that, and I'm not sure I could stand to be that close to him and not act on my desires. I could be setting myself up for disappointment if I jump into this thinking it might mean a job *and* a guy, only to find out the guy isn't available.

Too bad Katah Vista's not bigger. It wouldn't matter if Blake and I aren't on the same page then. However, in a town that size, we're likely to run into each other daily. It's the only downside I can think of to this whole coaching thing. But knowing a move like this will put us in each other's orbit on the regular, something that could make us both miserable if we don't want the same thing, it doesn't feel right to commit without getting his take. I should probably test things out first, but I can't deny I'm tempted to do whatever is necessary to convince him this is a good idea.

"I'm interested," I tell Axel as he finishes his pitch, "but I want to check it out before I decide. If I'm going to park myself in one place, I need to get out of my trailer, and I'm not living with you and Lennon," I cut him off before he can offer. "Let me check out the area and this barn to see how much work it's really gonna be. Then I'll let you know."

"I'll tell Lennon you're coming." He grins like I've already said yes, and I roll my eyes to hide the fact that he's probably right.

***

The waiting room could use a facelift. Not only is it beige on top of beige, but the chairs look like they were made in the eighties, complete with worn fabric stretched thin between two rickety arm rests. It's definitely not the relaxing, rejuvenating experience the sign out front promises.

A bored-looking brunette looks up from her phone when I enter. "Can I help you?"

"Jace Anderson, I have an appointment." I step to the counter to sign in and she hands me a clipboard with some forms. When I've finished them, she leads me to a changing room where she instructs me to lock up my clothes and valuables and don a robe. After I change, she escorts me to a lounge and tells me to wait here until I'm called.

The lounge at least has some windows, offering a decent view of the highest peak at the resort. This time of year it's a vibrant green, thanks to a good snowfall over the winter, with patches of wildflowers dotting the slope. I take a seat—the leather couches in here make up for the dated reception area—and flip through a magazine, some cigar thing that smells sort of woodsy. Like cedar. At least flowers and makeup aren't the only reading material.

Finding nothing of interest, I toss it on the coffee table as a heavy door whooshes open. Blake pauses mid-stride when his gaze settles on me, his eyes growing wide a half-second before they glaze with heat.

I know the feeling; you do the same thing to me. It's a heady sensation to know I have such an effect on him, and my cock swells under the robe in response.

"I thought I'd take you up on that massage." I break the silence, my eyes tracking over his sculpted frame, which is evident despite the generic uniform of khaki pants and a polo with the resort logo.

He references the clipboard, swallowing audibly. "My chart says Anderson, not Jace."

"Anderson is my last name. I wanted to surprise you."

"Yeah?" A hint of a smile ghosts across his face.

"Yeah. I wanted to see your reaction when you realized I was here."

"Why?" He licks his lips, and my dick strains under the heavy fabric.

"To make sure you're happy to see me." I stand and cross the room until we're a few feet apart.

"Why wouldn't I be?" His eyes grow hooded as he notices the lump under my robe, and he not so subtly adjusts his own bulge.

"We didn't make plans. I wasn't sure if this would be overstepping or not." I fist my hands by my side to keep from reaching for him.

He takes a shaky breath. "It's definitely not overstepping. Let's get you into a room before these boners get me fired." He opens the lounge door and holds it ajar for me to pass through. I let my hand brush over his dick as I walk by, biting my lip to hold in a groan when I hear his.

Blake guides me down the hall to a small room with a long, padded table in the center. I stand facing the foot of the table as he closes the door and turns on some sort of elevator music, upping the volume a few notches. Then I feel him close the distance between us, so he's pressed behind me.

Taking my chin in one hand he turns my head and devours my mouth while the other yanks the robe off and cups my dick, giving it a long, slow pull. My body barely has time to register the spike in pleasure before he lets go and growls, "On the table. Face down."

I don't know if it's because we're on his turf or because he really is happy to see me, but 'Take-Charge Blake' has my tip leaking with anticipation. Right up until his words register. "Face down?" I choke, looking at my engorged boner. "I'm not sure that's an option."

"You want the full massage experience?" He cocks an eyebrow. "Lie down."

Cupping my dick to my belly, I climb on the table, gingerly trapping my erection between my body and the sheet beneath me. As soon as I'm situated with my forehead resting on the hollow little pillow Blake covers me with a blanket. I hear the telltale suction of a bottle returning to its original shape, then hands rubbing together. Warm palms hit my skin, sending a jolt of pleasure straight to my cock. It takes all my energy not to rut my hips against the table to relieve the pressure, and for a moment, I worry that he's got me so aroused I won't last more than a few seconds even though he's not touching my dick. Then he hits a knot in my shoulders, and my body seems to deflate.

Strong fingers knead along my neck, my spine, my back, turning rigid muscle to jelly. As Blake drives the tension from my body, he lulls me into a boneless state. One where my lust simmers beneath the surface without demanding to be satisfied. A suspended euphoria, if you will. His hands coast over my skin, alternately kneading and caressing my tired limbs. *Fucking hell, he's good at this.*

When he's done with my back, Blake works his way down to my legs, rubbing the length of my hamstrings from the back of my knee to my ass, which he molds in his strong hands. Every once in a while, his fingers lightly graze over my hole, promising more to come. The combination of soft and hard pressure has my cock growing firm, and just when I'm ready to demand he stop teasing me he drifts to my calves and feet, making my body limp all over again.

Alternating between frustrated and relaxed is weird as fuck, but I kind of like it, since it sort of heightens my senses, making every touch electric. I'm thinking of ways I can give him the same experience when his deep voice rumbles behind my ear. "Flip over."

I roll to my back, freeing my cock to stand tall and proud as much as it can underneath the blanket, which hinders but doesn't hide my arousal. Then Blake starts the process over again, working my head and neck, my shoulders, and my chest. His capable hands leave no part of my body untouched, except for the one spot where I need it most.

Eventually, he makes his way to my legs. Working each one at a time, he lifts the blanket off the leg he's concentrating on so that it's exposed while my boner is still covered. As he works my quads his fingers brush my sac, making my dick twitch under the blanket. I see him lick his lips as he takes note of the way my cock strains, but he doesn't touch it. Not until he's massaged everywhere else.

Once he's rubbed out every knot, Blake finally, *finally*, lifts the blanket off me. With his heated eyes focused on my dick he squirts some oil on his hands and rubs his palms together, then clasps me in both fists.

He squeezes and pulls up my shaft, alternating hands so my entire length is constantly covered by his expert fingers. My eyes roll back in my head as my hips lift, chasing his grip. Then he wraps both hands around me and gently twists his wrists in opposite directions before pulling on my shaft again.

Over and over, he switches between twisting and tugging on my cock, firm enough to feel the pressure without causing any pain. I've never had my dick worked so thoroughly before, and it's fucking intense. I'm torn between prolonging the pleasure and tipping over the edge, both options sounding really fucking good. I can *feel* how hard I am in his hand, how heavy my balls are, and I press my hands against the table for leverage as I tilt my hips, pushing into his grip.

"Your dick is so swollen right now," Blake pants. "I can't stand it." He lets me go long enough to unzip his pants and fish his own bulging cock out as he reaches for a condom.

"Take your shirt off," I plead between heaving breaths. "I want to see your body while you fuck me."

Blake yanks his shirt over his head, giving me a tantalizing glimpse of the lean hips that rut forward when he fists his dick. Biceps flexing with barely contained restraint, he wraps up and dribbles more oil over the condom.

"Don't make a sound," he growls as he pushes his tip in my hole. Despite gritting my teeth so hard I feel like they'll crack, a guttural moan rumbles up my throat. "I mean it, keep quiet." Blake warns as he wraps a hand around my cock, thrusting in rhythm to the hand pumping my length.

Still somewhat boneless from the massage, I can do little else but lie motionless as Blake drives into me, fast enough that my body shifts on the table but with enough restraint that our skin doesn't smack together. *Thank God he's in charge, because I'm about as useful as a bowl of Jello.*

Hard, deep, bordering on frantic, whether due to raw desire or the need to finish before we're caught, Blake drives us toward a punishing release. I take everything he has to give, offering him total control of my body. He takes it willingly, the round head of his cock jackhammering my prostate so relentlessly I'm teetering on the edge within minutes. Maybe even seconds.

Between the subtle touches that elicit a warm current of electricity, and the powerful grip of Blake's hand on my junk as he fucks into me, my nerves are overloaded. The pleasure's too much. I can't hold back. Clenching my teeth, I hold my breath as cum shoots out of me, coating my stomach, my chest, and nearly reaching my chin. Blake licks his lips as he watches me paint myself with my release, then he throws his head back, the tendons in his neck straining just under the skin as he empties into me with a barely contained groan.

Chapter 9

Blake

Holy Shit! When I finally regain control of my body, I bring my head forward and find Jace staring at me intently, his breath as ragged as mine.

We watch each other for a moment as we recover, something we didn't get to do in the dim light of his hotel room. Milky white liquid is splattered over his torso. His skin glistens from a combination of sweat and the oil I rubbed him with, highlighting the peaks and valleys of his muscular abdomen, the trail of hair leading to the cock I still have in hand. I give it a gentle squeeze as I stare into the dark abyss of his soulful eyes, which never leave mine. It's… Shit, it's kind of perfect, both of us sweaty and sated and *not*. Like we both sense this isn't over, and we don't want it to be.

"That was…"

"Yeah." I grip the base of my dick, so I don't lose the condom and slide out, tossing it in the trash as I grab a towel off the counter. Turning to Jace, I wipe his cum off him and hand him the robe I left pooled on the floor.

"How long are you in town for?" It's a lame question after the intensity of what we just did, but now that we aren't connected, part of me wonders if I'm the only one that felt it. Acting casual feels like the safest thing to do right now.

Jace shrugs on the robe as I put my junk away and stick my arms through the sleeves of my shirt. "I don't know yet. Could be a few days, could be a helluva lot longer."

I pause with my shirt midway to my head. "Seriously?"

"Yeah." Jace casts me a tentative smile as he runs his hand through his hair. "Axel's all in with Lennon—bought property and everything—and he's got this plan to run some sort of training camp for kids in between competitions. He wants me to help him with it."

My lips threaten to crack into a smile, so I tug the shirt over my head before he can see it. The last thing I want to do is scare him off. "Think you're gonna do it?"

"Maybe." His eyes are glued to the belt on the robe as he twirls it in his fingers. "That's actually why I'm here. I need to go over the plan, take a look at the property he has in mind. Get your thoughts..." His gaze snaps to mine.

"Mine?" I point to my chest.

"This is your turf." He lifts a shoulder. "I wasn't sure how cool you'd be with me coming here."

My turf? I cross my arms over my chest and stare him down, feeling betrayed. "What are you trying to say? That I don't want any competition for dudes?"

He shakes his head slowly back and forth. "I'm saying I didn't want you to think I'd expect anything from you if I move here. But if I do, well, I'm into the idea of being close to a guy who gets all sides of me. I don't know what that means or what it would look like, but I'm down to figure that out. If you are."

Holy Shit. "Are you saying you want to date?" Despite wishing for more after our last encounter, I wasn't really expecting it to happen, least of all a week later.

Jace licks his lips appreciatively. It's sexy, although I'm not sure he means it to be. "I don't know," he says as he sits back down on the table. "I haven't been in one place long enough to date anyone, and you're pretty private when it comes to this." He draws an imaginary line between the two of us. "But if I live here, I'd want to see you."

"Yeah?" It's damn near impossible to keep the grin off my face. *I can't believe this is happening.* After walking away from him, and then Becca, I was starting to wonder if I was going to be single forever. Now that Jace is here, suggesting something more than a casual fuck... It feels like things are falling into place, just like I held out hope they would one day.

"You are kind of the only dude I know here, except for Axel." Jace brings me back to our conversation. "And besides, you're a great fuck." He shoots me a sly grin as his eyes take an exaggerated tour of my body.

I can't help laughing at his obvious attempt to play it cool. "So, you want my dick?"

"Obviously." He gives me a mock eye roll. "But I'd like someone to hang out with, too. If you're cool with that. We can figure the other shit out as we go, right?"

Jace reaches for my hand, the same sweet gesture he made that first night when we were talking about how we live our lives, and a stark contrast from his typically confident persona. It makes me wonder if he feels starved for affection, too. I guess I assumed since he has Axel, his situation might be better somehow. But right now, with our fingers linked together, I get the sense there's a part of him that wants more than just someone to talk to.

"Have you got a place to stay tonight?" My voice sounds almost raspy as he runs his thumb along mine.

"Are you offering?" He tilts his head up to meet my gaze.

"I am. As long as you don't have other plans."

"That won't cause issues for you? Small town talk and all?" He bites the corner of his lip, not quite hiding the ghost of a smile that tugs at it.

"I've got a spare room," I trail off.

"That you're offering to let a friend crash in while he's visiting?" He finishes my thought, and before I can question whether the ruse might offend him, he gives my hand a little tug, pulling me toward him.

"Something like that." I step between his legs. "And we'll figure out the rest as we go, right?"

"Right." Jace brushes his lips across mine, so softly I almost wonder if I imagined it. Then he pulls back and locks his dark, heated gaze on mine. "Take me home."

***

Jace heads back to the changing room to get dressed while I clean up, then I meet him in the parking lot out back.

"Should I follow you to your place or...?" He trails off when I walk to the passenger side of his truck.

"I'll just ride with you since I don't have a car here."

"You don't have a car?" he asks as I hear the lock click open.

"I do, but I only drive it when I need to go somewhere the bus doesn't."

"The bus?" Jace wrinkles his nose as he turns the ignition over. "Why would you ever pick the bus over your own ride?"

"Don't knock it 'til you try it. It runs every fifteen minutes, goes everywhere I do, and it's free. Left here." I point in the direction we need to go as Jace pulls out of the lot.

"I can't imagine not having the freedom to go wherever I want, whenever I want."

"That's because you live and work on wheels. Move here, I bet I'll convert you in three months' time."

He shakes his head despite the hint of a smile on his face. "Good luck with that."

As we make the ten-minute drive from the mountain to my house, I point out different landmarks, like the first house built in town, the gas station that just happens to have some of the best breakfast sandwiches, and the bus stop closest to my house—so he knows how to get around without his truck. Then I guide him to the driveway of the little bungalow I call home.

"It's not much, but I don't have to worry about it rolling away if I forget to put the parking brake on." I give him a playful wink as I climb out of the cab.

"Don't knock the trailer 'til you've tried it." He snorts as he pulls a duffel bag from the back. "There's nothing quite like sleeping next to the best outdoor playgrounds on the planet."

"Why do you think I've never left this place?" I sweep my arm out as I spin around, gesturing to the towering peaks around us.

"Show off," he mumbles as he follows me to the door, it sounds like he's fighting a laugh as he says it. "So, I guess if you're still at the spa, the bike thing didn't pan out?" Jace sets his bag in the foyer.

"Actually, no. This is my last week at the spa. I'm starting at the resort full-time on Monday."

"That's great," he says as he takes in his surroundings, which don't amount to much. A small entry nook, a great room, a kitchen to our left and a hallway with bedrooms to our right. "What are the plans for the park."

I gesture for him to follow me and head to the kitchen. "That'll be up to my new boss." I pull two beers from the fridge and hand him one. "I've never built a bike park and it's too big of a project for me to run given my lack of experience, so they're bringing in someone that's done it before."

"So, what's your role, then?" He cracks open the can and takes a sip.

I wipe a dab of foam from my lip. "Project Manager. Or something to that effect. I'm supposed to coordinate with the suppliers, since I know them all, to help the new guy get whatever he needs."

"Sounds like a good gig."

"I hope so."

"You don't sound so sure." Jace's head tilts to the side as he studies me. I didn't even realize my voice shifted, and I don't know if it's good or bad that he picked up on it.

"I am sure, at least for now. I don't know if it'll be a full-time thing once it's built, and I'd really like it to be. But I'm probably getting ahead of myself."

Jace rests his forearms on the counter, the fingers of his right hand toying with the tab on the can. "I might be getting ahead of myself too... But if this thing with Axel pans out, maybe he'll need people with biking experience. You could work there when you aren't at the resort."

"My experience isn't on bikes with motors." I toss him a wry grin. "And besides, I'd hardly need a backup job during the summer when I actually have a job."

"Yeah, I guess it's not an exact fit. Told you I was probably thinking too much." He lifts his shoulders in a little half shrug as his cheeks flush with color. *God, he's cute.* "I just hate the idea of you not working with bikes full-time since you love it so much."

"I'm sure it'll all work out somehow."

"Eventually, yeah," he agrees, casting me a curious look when I choke back an awkward laugh.

"We're already making a mess of the figuring stuff out as we go thing, huh? I mean, you trying to hook me up with a job I may not need isn't exactly taking shit one day at a time."

He fights a smile as my words register. "New job opportunities, new... *rooming arrangements.* Maybe I'm trying too hard at this seeing someone thing." He resumes fiddling with his beer can.

"Does that mean you're having second thoughts about staying in town?"

"Fuck no. I'm looking forward to that part." His eyes dart briefly to mine before dropping back to the can in his hands. "It's just, you know, you're helping me out with a place to stay, and I want to help you out with a job, if that's what you need."

"Offering you a place to stay was self-serving." I pull his hand off his beer and thread our fingers together.

"So is me trying to help you with a job."

"How do you figure?"

"I'd rather have you working close to me than at the spa."

I drop his hand like a hot potato. "You wouldn't trust me to work there?"

He snatches my hand back and tugs it toward to his chest, bringing our faces closer together. "I don't trust other people not to hit on you—you're too hot. But I didn't say I don't want you working at the spa. I said I want you working closer to me. If that's an option."

My heart thumps heavily inside my chest. *Damn this is moving fast, but I kind of like it.*

"So, you're the possessive type?" I'm helpless to stop the grin from spreading across my face.

"Apparently." He grabs the back of my head with his free hand and presses his lips to mine. "Now, show me where I'm gonna be sleeping."

Chapter 10

Jace

"This is it." Axel beams proudly as I pull up to the address he gave me and step out of the truck.

Eyes hidden behind my shades; I spin around taking in the property. A large house sits directly in front of me, and there's a massive barn off to the side, slightly behind it. It's situated in a way that I doubt you can even see it from the house, since the attached garage would block the view, and the back of the house is angled away from the barn. Not that the giant horse house is an eyesore. It might be the general shape of a barn, with a pointy roofline that tapers down the further you get from the center, but it's elongated rather than being strictly triangular, and it's not painted bright red. It's more of a modern-looking dark wood with even darker trim, same as the house. Not quite contemporary, but not full-on country either.

The land itself is sprawling, with wild grass growing over gently rolling hills until it meets the treeline at the edge of the property. It's sort of ideal as far as location goes, because bikes are loud as fuck, and there's not another house in sight. I wonder if there are any trails in the trees. And the barn looks sizeable enough from the outside, but that's not exactly a green light.

"What do you think?" Axel's voice is tinged with excitement.

"Seems like a great spot." I turn my gaze back to the barn. "But we both know this was built for horses, not bikes. What do you have to do to get it ready?"

I follow Axel toward the large doors as he rattles a list over his shoulder. "Tear out the horse stalls, truck in more dirt, frame in a break room and maybe even a bunk area if we offer overnight camps—fortunately there's already plumbing since there's a bathroom inside—and hopefully there's enough room left over to put in a foam pit to practice jumps."

The massive doors swing open to reveal a mostly blank canvas of dirt. It wouldn't be impressive if you didn't make your living playing in it, but it's hard not to catch Axel's excitement now that I've seen it.

Aside from a corner in the back that's framed in to house the existing bathroom, and some sort of small office, the entire space is not only wide open but tall.Tall enough to build a launch point where you could throw jumps. Even better, the exposed rafters might support a harness that would let us suspend a rider if it looks like they won't land a jump they're attempting. Between that and a foam pit, there's no safer way to practice the complex tricks that win competitions.

"I haven't had the electricity turned on yet, but hopefully, the windows let in enough light for you to get the idea."

Axel follows behind me as I prop my shades on top of my head and venture inside. He can't see the way my jaw drops to the floor as I envision what this place would look like finished. "Can you imagine if we had a space like this to train in growing up? We'd... Well, you'd still be you, only better, and I'd have probably mastered that Cliffhanger," I refer to the trick that ended my riding career when I wasn't able to land it.

"You didn't master the Cliffhanger because you were more interested in your cameras than your bike." Leave it to my de facto brother to give me a healthy dose of reality. He's not wrong. Although we met in the sport and eventually started training together when he moved in with us to get away from his rough home life, Axel spent his free time on his bike while I spent mine fiddling with camera equipment. That's why he's the pro and I'm the cameraman. I'm not complaining—I love what I do. But I can't help wondering if I'd have achieved more with more resources.

"And we did have something similar to this," Axel interrupts my ride down memory lane. "You remember the place that used to be a gymnastics studio? I used to beg your dad to take us every Sunday to practice jumps in that foam pit."

"We had to drive three towns over and rent time." I point out as I walk the perimeter, mentally cataloging how to fit all the features on Axel's list. "And it wasn't a sleepover camp like you're talking about."

"So, if there was a camp like this when we were learning you would've gone to it?"

"Hell yeah."

"Then you're in? You'll help me make it happen?" Axel shoots a smile that says he already knows my answer, and while it's tempting to say I'll build something the younger me would've loved, I'm not ready to say yes. Putting my initial excitement aside, I have no idea what this endeavor entails. Would it be full-time or part-time? Would I still have the freedom to travel to film, if I don't want to give that up? Could I make a living teaching kids how to ride?

He must sense my hesitation because he plows ahead. "Wouldn't it be cool to live in one spot for a while? I know you know how lonely it can get on the road." He doesn't add the part about him not being there, but we're both thinking it. We've been traveling together for too long not to.

"You aren't obligated to domesticate me just because you've taken the plunge," I retort, even though my mind has already wandered in that direction with Blake. Normally, I wouldn't hide something like that from my best friend, but since Blake's still in the closet, it's not fair of me to out him. "Besides, I don't see how I'd be any less lonely here than on the road, considering you'll be spending all your free time with Lennon."

"My bad. I guess I figured you might've already found someone to hang out with." He holds his hands up in a *surrender* pose, like there isn't a deeper meaning behind his words.

"What?" I will my face to stay expressionless since my eyes aren't hidden behind my sunglasses.

"You think I didn't notice you eying Blake when you first saw him?" Axel arches a knowing brow. "Bet you already took him up on that massage. Maybe even more, seeing as how you *"rolled into town"* this morning instead of last night." He makes these ridiculous air quotes as he bates me, clearly well aware of my fib about arriving just now. *Stupid small towns.*

"Keep that to yourself," I hiss, my eyes darting around the room involuntarily to make sure we're alone even though I know we are. "Blake's not out yet."

Axel purses his lips and makes a low whistle. "You sure you want to take that on?"

"It's not a deal breaker." I shrug my shoulders with more indifference than I feel. Rushing Blake is the last thing I want to do, and while I'm not keen on taking a step back by hiding the truth, I'm willing to do that while he warms up to the idea of coming out.

"I hear you." Axel holds my gaze in his as he nods, a silent message that he won't spill Blake's secrets. "But from what I know of this town, it's too small and tight knit to keep secrets. Seeing him won't be an easy thing to keep quiet, and if he's determined to stay closeted, well, I don't want you to get hurt because he's not in a place where he can be all in."

"Don't get ahead of yourself." I clap him on the shoulder. "Hooking up doesn't mean either of us is all in." The words spill off my tongue with ease, though they won't stop replaying in my mind. *We talked about figuring it out as we go. You don't say that unless you want to make something work, right?*

"Yeah, okay," Axel sighs. "For what it's worth, I like Blake. A lot. I just don't want his secrets to dictate how you exist in this town."

"You're sure I'm going to agree to stay?"

"We haven't lived apart for over ten years now," he retorts, referencing everything from living together as kids to traveling together as part of the dirt bike circuit. "At this point I don't think you know how to survive without me."

"Yeah, which is why *you* are so desperate for *me* to come help you out."

"Good help is hard to find," he dismisses my comment the way only a brother can.

"And you need that help to do what exactly? I'm still not clear on that part." I cross my arms in front of my chest and arch my brows, waiting. This ought to be good since Axel is more of a show up where you tell me to kind of guy.

"Uh, anything and everything." He runs a hand through his disheveled blond hair. "I've got contractors to do all the building stuff, and I'm solid on doing the training part, but as far as turning it into a working business I'm not really sure where to start."

"You want me to be a desk guy?" My jaw falls halfway to the floor.

"It's not like you don't sit at a desk and watch film and shit all the time," he deadpans, as if that makes perfect sense.

"Yeah—After I've been out filming it. I don't... Hey, what if you film the kids who come to train? It could be a teaching tool and a souvenir."

"Ooh, that's good. Maybe you can even teach some kids how to film if they're interested in that."

"That's good, too," I agree. "But I'm not a desk guy. I don't do legal shit and I sure as hell don't do numbers. You gotta hire someone for that."

"Fine, but you already do all the scheduling with sponsors and manage the logistics of moving the crew from event to event, so can't you do stuff like that for the kids?" His puppy dog eyes had a greater impact on me when we were kids, and I sort of considered him my first guy crush, but even though he's more brother than friend now I still can't say no to the fucker, and he knows it.

I rub my hand over my face with a pained groan. "I really should make you do this yourself but since I have a feeling you don't know what you don't know, I'll stick around and help you figure it out. For now."

The grin that spreads across his face rivals the one wore when he won his last competition. This must really mean a lot to him.

Axel holds his fist out for me to bump it. "It's a good idea though, right? We can retire from biking without retiring from biking."

I don't have the heart to tell him that I could stay filming in the industry a lot longer than he could stay riding in it. Instead, I say, "Yeah. It's a good idea."

***

After telling Blake about my day, and how I'm going to stay at least for a little while to see what sort of potential is in this bike training thing, I bury myself inside him until we're both sated and spent. That's when Axel's warning about secrets impacting my life comes back.

I meant what I said about not rushing Blake into exposing a side of himself he's not ready for other people to know about. No matter how much you speculate or try to predict the outcome, you can never really anticipate how people will react. There's a certain comfort in never having to find out what the reality would look like. And if the reality that follows him revealing his truth isn't what he expected... Well, I'd hate for him to feel like he was forced into coming out and regret it. I won't be that guy. But given how easy things seem between us, I don't want to find myself in a situation where I'm Blake's dirty little secret, either.

While I may not be shouting about my sexuality from the rooftops, that doesn't mean I'm hiding or ashamed of it. I don't make it a point to label myself when the people I sleep with have no bearing on who I am as a person, but if anyone does label me, I'm comfortable with that. It doesn't change who I am or how my closest friends and family see me, but that's because I don't have secrets from them.

Back when I was in Blake's shoes, I remember feeling uncertain. I had to work up to a point where I felt ready to come out, and until I got there myself, nothing anyone said or did would have altered the timeline. Just like with any other big change in life, the only person who can tell you you're ready for it is you. I know that better than anyone. Unfortunately, that doesn't make it any easier to stomach the idea of trying to date someone you can't acknowledge you're dating.

I've heard horror stories about that; one guy being out while the other is still in the closet. The sneaking around, the lies that inevitably come with the secrecy, it wears on you, spoiling everything. That alone should be a red flag with Blake, but I don't want to stop this before knowing if it could be genuine. Not when I feel a connection to him unlike anything I've experienced with another man. That said, I have no desire to live in the shadows. I'm willing to do it up to a point, if only to see how real this can be. But I'd need to know there's an end in sight. Knowing why he's still in the closet—the real reason, not just the label thing—would go a long way towards making me feel comfortable with his secrecy.

"Can I ask you a question?" I prop myself on an arm so I can face him lying next to me.

"Sure."

"Why do you really keep your interest in guys private?"

A tiny line appears between his brows. "I told you, people talk in a small town, and I don't want the extra attention."

"Yeah." I brush a strand of hair away from his face, something I can't seem to stop myself from doing. "But you also talk about how much you love this place and the people here, and I'm not really following how you can feel at home here and not be yourself at the same time."

He chews on his lip while staring at the ceiling for so long I start to think he won't answer. Then he takes a deep breath. "I'm not afraid of people knowing I like guys, but I don't know what they'd think about the bi thing. Even I have trouble wrapping my brain around it sometimes. I used to get so confused because I didn't know it was possible to like both, so I'd go back and forth between liking men or women, thinking I had to pick one. By the time I realized I didn't have to choose, I'd spent so long being lost I just figured it would be easier to keep things to myself than explain it over and over again. That's why I never dated or hooked up publicly." His arm muscles twitch as he makes a fist in the comforter. "I mean... I don't want to be single forever, and I always figured when I found *"the one"* it would make the choice for me. Sort of like a sign from the universe or whatever. If that was a woman, I wouldn't have to say anything, just do the whole marriage and family thing. If it was a man, I'd come out as gay. That just seemed... *simpler*."

"*The one*," I repeat his words. "Does that mean you've never had a thing for anyone? Guy or girl?"

"You're the only guy I've been with more than once." His eyes dart bashfully to mine before focusing back on the ceiling.

"No women?" I prompt.

"There was one who I thought maybe... I haven't seen her since, though. What about you?" He wets his lips nervously.

"Same as you, really." I trace his collarbone with my fingertip. "There was one woman who made a lasting impression, and I always hoped I'd see her again one day, but I haven't. Then I met you, and you also made a lasting impression."

His cheeks flush the most beautiful shade of pink.

"I'm curious," I continue, still teasing my fingers over his skin, "you mentioned the *simple* solution being a man or a woman. Does that mean you're planning to stick to one or the other forever? Do you think you could?" I've never asked myself that question, but I also never went through a period of thinking I'd have to choose. I wonder if dating might change that.

He turns his head to face me. "I can be monogamous, if that's what you're getting at."

"It wasn't, but I like the idea that we don't sleep with other guys. I'm more curious how to keep this," I cup his dick in my palm, "between us if I'm not just visiting and you're not ready to come out. It's not like I can make appointments at the spa since you're not going to work there anymore, and constantly being at each other's places would start rumors, right?"

He lets out a ragged breath as I give him a firm squeeze before releasing him. "I do have that spare room."

"We just agreed yesterday to see how things go and you want to move in together?" It's hard to keep the surprise out of my voice.

Blake runs a hand over his face. "You're right, sorry. Bad idea."

"Well, maybe not." I run my fingertip along his arm. "It would give us a cover story while we see where things go."

"Roommates?" His forehead creases with uncertainty.

"Unless you're ready to come out." I lift my shoulder, trying to appear indifferent so he doesn't feel like he has to take cues from me and how I live my life.

Blake gnaws on his lip before turning his wary eyes on me. "Does it make me sound like I'm not into this if I say no? Because I am. Into this, I mean."

"I know." I plant a soft kiss on his lips, hoping to reassure him that I understand even if I don't share his hesitation. "Like I said, we'll figure it out as we go. For now, we'll go with roommates."

Blake cracks a relieved smile. "When do you move in?"

"Next week? I don't have much but it's all in my trailer, which is still parked near our last event in New Mexico. I'll have to drive there and... Shit." I flop back on the pillow, overwhelmed with the logistics of *settling down.*

"What?" Blake reaches for my hand.

"I have no idea what to do with my trailer. I'm usually always in it so I don't have a place to store it. Even if I did, it's where I keep all my camera equipment, so I don't want to just leave it anywhere." There's also the issue of whether I'll even need it going forward if Axel retires and we stop traveling the country for events. Not that his retirement automatically triggers mine, but if this new idea he has pans out and I stay here...

"Couldn't you park it at Axel's place? He's got a lot of land, right?" Blake's question saves me from spiraling too deep in my head.

"That's a thought. It'd be close enough I could have access to any camera stuff I need but still be out of the way since the property is so big. I could get it and be back within a week."

He gives my hand a squeeze. "I'd offer to help but the guy Jackson recommended for the bike park is due in at the end of the week, and I assume we'll jump right in to developing it. I need to be here for that."

"You definitely shouldn't miss your new boss. And I'll probably get back faster if you aren't slowing me down."

"How would I slow you down?" Blake's mouth parts in astonishment, and even though it's not meant to be sexy it makes my mind wander to where else I'd like to see his mouth.

"By looking so fucking hot I can't concentrate." I rub my thumb over his plump lip.

"When you put it that way." He sucks my thumb between his lips, waking my spent cock. We take advantage of the rest of the night, giving me a proper sendoff.

Chapter 11

Becca

Spinning around to get my bearings, I can't help but notice the three-hundred-sixty-degree view of the mountains in my new hometown. Back in Utah, which has its own fair share of beautiful peaks, the only mountains were to the east. Here, they're everywhere you look. It's familiar yet not, which sort of makes me giddy.

When I got the call about a job building a bike resort, I wavered about whether to accept. Not that I was intimidated by the job or the move, I just wasn't sure anywhere else could compare to Utah. And that was a problem, seeing as how my life there was running on autopilot. Certain aspects of it, anyway.

While I loved my job, my boss, and the mountain itself, I had no life outside that tiny little bubble. That's partly because I allowed myself to retreat into workaholic mode after my breakup, and partly because I'd always been so passionate about what I did that I didn't do a great job of making friends, and that was before I used my breakup as an excuse to work more. Staying there wouldn't have been miserable, but it would've been a crutch. So, I decided to challenge myself with a new beginning, and if this view is any indication, my fresh start is going to be epic!

It's not hard to see why Katah Vista works as a ski resort. The rolling hills that spill into the base area are framed by towering peaks, which undoubtedly offer a great selection of green, blue and black runs in the winter. In the late summer, wildflowers dot the landscape with pops of red, yellow, and purple rising up the slope of the hill to break up the lush green grass. I make a note to preserve as much of that natural growth as possible when defining the routes for the bike trails.

Aside from the odd hiker winding their way up the mountain, there's not much activity here. That's a stark contrast from what I'm used to. In Utah, the chairs start spinning at nine, and bikers are lined up for close to thirty yards as they wait their turn to load their bikes and ride to the top. There's a sort of restless tension that ripples through the line as everyone watches the clock, absently bouncing on the balls of their feet or rolling their bike back and forth with nervous excitement. When the mountain opens, the first riders come down the hill with high-fives and fist pumps and whoops of joy as people roll to the back of the line to do it again.

It's strange to see a place capable of that same atmosphere being so quiet, and while I'm committed to building the best park I can, if the goal is to increase summertime revenues, I'll be able to do that without even trying.

I'm halfway to the administrative offices, daydreaming about what this place could look like next summer, when I spot a guy in a suit making his way toward me. I know without a doubt this is Carter, my new boss, because who besides the owner would wear a suit in a place like this? *Good thing I'm not a suit girl or I'd find him seriously distracting. Dark hair, square jaw, broad shoulders—who knew a man could make them look this good?*

"Becca." He extends his hand with a warm smile. "I'm so glad you could make it on such short notice. Did you get settled in okay?"

I nod as his hand closes around mine. "Yes, thank you. And thanks for giving me a room at the resort until I find a place of my own."

"It's no trouble. We're just excited to have you here. Jackson said you were instrumental in building the bike park in Utah, and I know it's one of the best in the country. We'd love to put something of that caliber here."

Shielding my eyes, I look up at the mountain. "You've certainly got the terrain for it. Have you given any thought to the plans I sent over?" Before accepting the position, I had Carter send over some aerial maps of the terrain, and a roughed out a few options for consideration.

"I have. I think it makes sense to do this in phases. Develop one section of the mountain and get it dialed in before moving to the next section. That way we're pulling in revenue even as we build out the rest of the park."

Straight to the point. I like it. "That was my thought, too," I agree, "and we can post signage advertising the future plans, so people make it a point to come back and try out the new terrain."

"Exactly." Carter's mouth spreads into a wide grin.

"I'd like to get on the mountain and check it out in person before we finalize anything, but I'm thinking we could start with some green runs because that mostly just involves moving dirt, not building any features. And personally, I find green runs a great option for all skill sets. Even if you're capable of something more difficult, it's still fun to glide down a flowy trail." I can't stop the giddy smile that spreads across my face as I think of my favorite green trail back home. I mean, back in Utah.

Carter laughs and shakes his head, apparently amused by my enthusiasm. "I'll take your word for it, but if that's the kind of face people make riding bikes, then I guess I have to try it."

I snap my jaw back in place—hopefully before he noticed that it fell open. "You're going all in on a bike park and you don't even ride?" *This, I was not expecting.*

"It makes sense for business." His tone seems to say *"duh."* "And most of my friends here are enthusiasts so it's a project they'll help support."

"Fair enough, although I'll hold you to trying it when it's finished." *He's gonna be so awed by the time I'm done.*

"Deal." Carter extends his hand again. "What can I do to help you get started?"

"Did you get the list of personnel and equipment requirements? Does that look okay?" Although some parts of the trail will have to be dug by hand to avoid disturbing the trees, other sections can be dug with a skid steer loader.

"I did, and my manager has been assembling everything on it."

"Manager?" My brows lift in surprise. I'm not opposed to having one, although I thought I'd be the one to hire him or her.

"Yes, Blake. He's a lifelong resident so he's well networked within the community. He's pulled together a team with decades of experience in trail management from the local parks and recreation department. They're all eager to get started. Just tell Blake what you need, and he'll take care of it." Carter lifts his eyes over my shoulder. "Here he is now."

Spinning in the direction of Carter's gaze, I turn to find the guy I picked up in the bar a few weeks back striding toward me, and a mixture of panic and excitement takes over my body. The rhythm of my heart turns erratic, my palms grow sweaty and it feels like someone has vacuumed the air from my lungs all at once. I'm not capable of doing anything beyond staying frozen in place. *Blake... Here?* Memories of our night bombard me, heating my cheeks, and I say a silent 'thank you' that my new boss is standing behind me so he can't see the way my eyes bug out.

There have only been two lovers I've fantasized about long after our time together, and the man closing in on me is one of them. Strong yet gentle, frenzied yet savoring... Blake made me feel desired and treasured, which is why I've replayed that night in my mind over and over again. Now, the object of those dreams is walking toward me? What are the odds? More importantly, are there rules about sleeping with your subordinate, or can that be overlooked since he wasn't technically working for me then? How do I explain this to Carter? Am I obligated to?

I start to tuck my hair behind my ear just to do something with my hands, only to remember it's tied back in a ponytail. It falls awkwardly to my side as I wait for the inevitable.

When he's about ten paces away, Blake's step falters slightly, realization sinking in, though his face remains expressionless. Still gorgeous, just blank. *That's some trick, I need to learn that.*

He offers me a hand as he closes the distance between us. *Ooh-does that mean we're going with strangers then?* "Blake," he says, formally clasping my hand as if he isn't already intimately familiar with it. And other...places. *Strangers it is.*

"Becca." It's a lost cause. One would think that having scratched the itch, per se would help keep the sparks floating between us at bay. One would be wrong. They're just as strong and unruly as they were when he caught me staring at him from across the bar. The second his hand closes around mine a current of electricity shoots up my arm, down to my stomach and into the *danger zone.*

"So, you're the one who helped Jackson build that bike park in Utah? I'm sorry I missed you when I was there."

I pull my hand back, so I have a chance at speaking coherently. "That's me." *Use more words, Becca.*

"Impressive." He nods methodically. "I got a chance to ride it briefly, and I can't tell you how excited I am about bringing something like that here."

"I'll leave you two to go over the plans and map out a schedule." Carter claps Blake on the back and gives me an encouraging nod before retreating to the administrative office. When he's out of sight, I turn a wary gaze to the man whose mere presence is making my heart race.

"So." I clap my hands together and rock back on my heels. "Fancy seeing you here." *Those are the best words you could find? You need help.*

Blake laughs, his hazel eyes showing a trace of mischief, which instantly relieves the pressure in my lungs. "Bec, I assume? What are the odds, huh?"

"Yeah, only Jackson really calls me that. And I literally just asked myself that same question." I exhale heavily, feeling a thousand percent less self-conscious. "So, is this cool? It's probably not too late for me to turn down the offer if this is too weird."

He rubs the bridge of his nose and sighs. "I think it kind of is. Besides, I'm assuming this is a pretty good opportunity for you, and I wouldn't want you to miss it on my account."

I wring my hands together just to give them something to do. "I do *really* want this job."

"And I want to bring a world class bike park to Katah Vista. Seems like a win, win. Right, boss?" Blake gives me a playful wink, and I say a silent prayer, hoping my face isn't on fire from the wandering direction of my thoughts. *I need to check on the fraternization rules.*

"It does." I smile so big my cheeks might crack, but I can't help it. My dream job and dream guy in one place? That's gotta be a sign or something. How did I get this lucky?

"Come on." He jerks his head toward a row of shops adjacent to the administrative building. "Let's grab a coffee and get started."

Coffees in hand, we pick a corner booth and I spread out some of the drawings I made to show Blake my ideas. Filling him in on the plan to build the park in stages, I point to a section on the rendering. "Do you think if we're merely cutting trail instead of building features we can crank these runs out before the season's over?"

"Are you hoping to make them ridable this summer?" His eyebrows disappear behind the hair hanging over his forehead as those blue eyes glint with excitement.

"Not for the general public, but we'll make sure everyone who helps build it gets a few runs in."

"A perk for a job well done?" A sly smile spreads across his lips.

"We can call it that." His boyish enthusiasm is catching. "Although, it's also a way for us to get feedback so we go into next summer knowing if we need to make any changes."

"Sounds like a plan. When do we start?"

"I still need to walk the terrain and verify that the routes I have mapped out will work, so... next week?" I bite my lip, wondering how feasible that schedule will be.

"Great. I'll line up the crew," he says without any hesitation, lifting another weight off my shoulders in the process. Unfortunately, the weight regarding our *situation* is still there, and aside from joking about the odds earlier he doesn't seem like he's going to address it. *I had to make the move the first time, guess I'll have to do it again.*

"So, what are you up to this evening?" I swirl my coffee cup in my hand to keep it busy.

"Uh." He looks everywhere but at me. "I'll uh, probably grab a bite then head home."

"Can I tag along?"

Blake ducks his head as he runs a hand over the back of his neck. "Sure. Yeah. Meet me at Murphy's on Main at seven." He collects our empty cups and tosses them in the trash, and with a tight-lipped smile and a nod he heads out the door.

Okay, that is not at all the reaction I expected.

The Blake I slept with is sensitive, gentle, and considerate. The Blake who just left is...*stiff*. I'm sure having me as his boss is a shock, but he seemed normal during that meeting, so why the hesitation about grabbing a bite? Does he not want a repeat of our night together? Obviously, we both expected that to be a one-time thing, though I got the impression it could be more if he wasn't just passing through. Did I misread him? Or worse, does he have a girl here and I'm an unwanted complication?

Normally, I wouldn't overanalyze like this, but Blake made me feel things I want to feel again. I didn't realize I missed the connection another person offers until I saw him face-to-face and recalled the sense of belonging I felt when I was with him. If he isn't thinking along those same lines, maybe the whole dream guy thing was premature? I guess I'll find out at dinner.

Chapter 12

Blake

Shit. *Shit.* My conscience wouldn't let me leave Becca alone on her first night in town, especially given our history. But our history means I know she's going to think dinner is just the start of the evening, and that's not good. Not now, when I've got a... *boyfriend*?

The word is strange inside my head, and I'm not sure if it's because we haven't referred to each other that way out loud or because it's the first time I've ever dated someone. Hell, it might be both. Either way, Becca's presence just got a lot more complicated.

Jace and I may both like women as well as men, but we haven't talked about whether it's okay to see them while we're seeing each other. Part of me thinks he'd be okay with it—he specifically said we shouldn't see other *guys*, which makes me wonder if girls are on the table. And if I want them to be.

When we talked about trying the whole dating thing, girls were nowhere on my radar. I wanted to give things with Jace a serious chance, and adding anyone to the mix, guy or girl, would only get in the way. I still believe that, mostly. It's only because the girl in question is Becca that I'm now confused as hell.

I felt an instant connection to her, same as I did with Jace, and if she had been the one to move here before he did... There's a very real chance I'd be trying to make a serious go of things with her, right now. Only she didn't show up first. He did, and even though it's still early on, things between us are really, *really* good.

It feels natural to fall asleep and wake up next to Jace. Talking to him comes so easily, which is a huge relief after years of guarding what I say. I don't want to give that up. I also don't want to hurt Becca, who also feels natural to be around. Though I don't have a commitment to her, she isn't a random hookup to me, and I don't want to do anything to give her that impression. Turning down any advances could have that effect, and based on past experience, she'll probably make an advance if I don't. Somehow, I have to get through dinner without hurting her. Or Jace.

From my perch on the barstool at Murphy's on Main—the new name since Lennon's planning to open a second location on the mountain—I see Becca the moment she steps inside. It's a busy night here—it always is during the summer tourist season—but her pink hair and bright smile make her stand out. It's both cute and hot at the same time, making my stomach do a little flip. *Dammit.*

How should I play this? Professional? Familiar? Smartass? What's the protocol for hanging out with your boss who you slept with and have to keep at arm's length even though you genuinely like her and maybe still want her a little? I went for professional earlier since we were talking about work, but I might've been sort of flirty to ease the tension. And I think I bordered on rude when she asked about dinner. I hardly remember at this point since my primary goal was not losing my shit. It still is. *Seriously, what are the odds?*

Becca spots me waving at the end of the bar and weaves her way through the crowd, heaving a sigh of relief as she takes the seat next to me. "Popular place." Her eyes are wide as she takes in the hum of activity.

"Best food in town. I usually try to avoid the dinner rush, but my boss had me lining up all sorts of people for this big project we've got going on, so I got stuck working late." I give her a little side eye as I sip my beer, hoping smartass is the right angle.

"Your boss sounds like a tyrant." Relief flows into my lungs as she matches my banter without any hesitation.

"Oh, she is. I mean, who makes you stay after five? Even if you're excited about the project and working on deadlines, five is the cutoff." I flag Lennon over before turning to look at Becca, who is grinning from ear to ear. "What can I get you to drink?"

"Um, a beer is fine."

"With that hair?" A deep voice rumbles from behind her. "No way, you need a—"

"Not another word, Deacon." I interrupt my very inappropriate friend before he can finish. "This is my boss. We don't play dirty drinks with her."

"Yeah, save the dirty drinks for The Underground. Murphy's is a family place." Lennon rolls her eyes at Deacon then wipes her hand on her apron and extends it to Becca. "The boss, huh? You'll fit right in. I'm Lennon. This not-so-suave idiot is Deacon." He grins salaciously and holds his hand out as well.

"Becca." She shakes both their hands. "Why will I fit in?" Her eyes dart between me, Lennon, and Deacon.

"I own this place, my friend Ally owns her clothes shop, Sloane runs her own physical therapy practice and Cora has her own consulting gig, although right now she's contracted to work for Carter."

"In other words, you're a badass." Deacon hovers near her ear. I shoot him a warning glare that he pretends not to notice.

"What does that make me?" Tiff materializes next to Lennon with a full pout on her lip. Good thing she's a sweetheart down deep or her unique ability to overhear conversations she's not part of would be pretty awkward.

"My trusty sidekick and also a badass," Lennon slings an arm around her shoulders and introduces her to Becca.

"And the dirty drink names?" Becca searches our faces for a hint.

Lennon puts a beer on the counter and points a finger at Deacon. "Be nice. And no dirty drinks in front of Tiff or her mom will kill me."

As soon as she's out of earshot, Tiff leans toward Becca so she doesn't have to shout. "It's a bar game where the guys string a bunch of dirty drink names together in a sentence. They use it to pick up girls."

"Does that work?" Becca wrinkles her nose.

"Let's just say this one has been around the world," she jerks her thumb toward Deacon, "without leaving Katah Vista."

"Tiff." Deacon puts a hand over his heart. "Don't sell me short. I've been around the world at least twice."

We all know he's exaggerating, but for a second I swear Tiff flinches. Then it's gone and her typical smile is back as she addresses Becca. "Deacon has a medical condition that gives him Blue Balls if he isn't Balls Deep in a Tight Snatch bringing Death to a Virgin at least five days a week. Was that better?" She blinks innocently at Deacon, whose jaw is hanging open.

"Four drinks. Nice." I give her a fist bump before she bounces off then turn to look at my burned friend over Becca's head. "And *that* is why Lennon doesn't want us playing dirty drinks in front of her. She's gonna take your title soon."

Shit! Becca. I risk a look at her, expecting to find a scowl of disgust on her usually happy face, only to find her nose buried in her phone. "What are you doing?"

"Looking up drinks. I'm going to school you both in this game." If that comment didn't come from underneath a mop of pink hair, I'd have thought it was straight from one of the guys.

I haven't seen this competitive side of her, but it makes my chest swell with pride as it sends a jolt of lust straight to my balls. *Fuck me.* How am I supposed to work side-by-side with someone I admire *and* want to sleep with? Again.

Deacon arches an impressed brow and looks at her phone over her shoulder. "This one should be your signature drink." He points at the screen.

"Pink Pany Dropper. No points for originality, but at least it looks refreshing."

I choke back a laugh as Deacon worms his way into the seat on the other side of Becca, which turns out to be a good thing since it makes things between her and I less *intimate*. Even though we're using dirty drink names to make ridiculous sentences.

Eventually, our conversation turns to the bike park, and we tell Deacon about our plan to build at least one green run before the summer ends. I had hoped that little teaser wouldn't get him too excited—there's still a lot that needs to fall perfectly into place to meet that timeline—but Becca's amped and he picks up on it. Only I'm not sure it's purely his excitement that has him hanging on her every word.

Becca isn't just beautiful in a casual, sporty kind of way, she lives and breathes biking, something most girls around here don't do. That combination is highly appealing, and I'm pretty sure if she weren't here with me Deacon would be making a move. Hell, he might do it anyway, thinking my hands are tied since she's my boss. And I don't like that one bit.

What's worse, Deacon isn't the only guy I'll have to worry about, he's just the most forward. Every single guy in town will be drawn to a gorgeous woman who can throw down on a bike, and there's not a damn thing I can do about it unless I want to risk things with Jace, which I absolutely don't want to do. How is this my life right now?

A few weeks ago, I felt grateful for the experience of meeting and sleeping with each one of them, separately. Now, I'm wondering how much it will hurt Becca to find out I've chosen Jace.

Wait a minute. She won't even know that, because no one does. No one will unless I come out of the closet, which I'll do if things with Jace keep going the way they are. Until then, Becca's probably going to think I just don't want *her*, which makes me sort of sick to my stomach.

Maybe being lonely was better, or at least it was less complicated.

Once we're done eating, Deacon heads off to The Underground, scouting for a hookup no doubt, although he promises to keep an eye out for Ryder since I'm sort of working.

I've barely seen my childhood best friend over the last week or so since my personal and professional life have suddenly become complicated, and I feel pretty shitty about that since his life came to a screeching halt about the same time. I make a mental note to check on him as soon as possible to see how he's doing without his brother as I settle the bill.

Outside, Becca and I make our way to the bus stop—the one she needs to head back to the resort is a different line than the one that goes to my house—and I'm hoping being on separate routes will make this a quick goodbye.

"You know which bus to take back to the resort, right?" I ask her as we take seats on a bench to wait.

"I do, although I was sort of thinking I didn't have to go there right away." She bites her lip in the most adorable way, and I have to grip the slats on the seat beneath me to keep from leaning toward her and taking it between my teeth.

Bracing for the worst, I take a cautious breath, which is probably the worst thing I could do.

"You don't feel the same." Her chest deflates as her gaze drops to the ground. *Shit.*

Knowing it's a risk, I loosen my grip on the bench and stretch my arm out, brushing my fingertips under her chin so she has to lift her head and meet my eyes. "Please don't think that. It's just... you're my boss now, and I want this job as much as you do. I don't want to cross any lines that shouldn't be crossed." *At least that's partly true.*

"Didn't we already do that?" she whispers.

"We could make that argument, but I'm not sure we should. We both have a lot riding on our jobs." The fact that our mutual boss, Carter, is dating a woman who used to work for him could come back to bite me since it suggests workplace romances are okay, but he is the friggin' owner of the resort and I'm not. That's what I'll say if she calls me on it.

"I guess that makes sense." Her shoulder rises listlessly. "And since we pretended to be strangers earlier today it would be awkward to try to explain we had a prior...whatever it was."

I'm both relieved and disappointed she's agreeing with me. But this is the right thing to do, and since I've already made a commitment to Jace it's the only solution. Still, I can't let her think that night wasn't important to me.

"It was incredible, Becca. One of the best nights of my life. Don't let the conflict we have now taint the memory of what we shared then."

"Um, wow. That was sort of beautiful." She blinks wide blue eyes up at me. It makes me feel even more like shit.

"See you at work tomorrow?" I give her a hand to help her rise as her bus pulls up to the stop.

"Deal." She takes it with a brave smile, then climbs inside without looking back. For the first time since Carter offered me this gig, I'm not looking forward to it.

Chapter 13

Jace

The last hour feels more like ten. That isn't a total shock—the last hour is always the longest—but it's never felt this long before. I think that's because I've never had anyone waiting for me at the end of the drive, and the anticipation of seeing Blake again has me on pins and needles.

Or maybe my ass is just asleep.

Pulling into the outskirts of town, my heartbeat accelerates, and my achy muscles itch to move. Although we've talked or texted every day, that didn't even begin to fill the void of not being able to see Blake's face or feel his body next to mine. *Is that a new relationship thing, or will coming home to him always feel like this?* I guess time will tell.

It's going on six when I finally pull into the drive after I drop my trailer at Axel's. Since the sun hasn't set there aren't any obvious signs that Blake is home, like lights glowing in the window. That kicks my heartbeat up another notch, and not in a good way. A mix of panic and dread floods my chest, and the idea that he might not be here makes me physically uneasy. And then the hum of the TV drifts toward me as I open the door, and the pressure in my chest subsides.

He's here.

Trying to ignore the mini breakdown I just experienced, I step inside and watch Blake, unnoticed, while I take a moment to get myself in check. His hazel eyes are unfocused as he flips aimlessly through the channels, so deep in thought the images on the screen don't seem to register.

I desperately want to know what's going on in his mind, but rather than intrude I stay still and let my eyes roam. There's a slight tension in his broad shoulders, a tiny crease between his brows, though he doesn't look mad, just serious. It's sort of hot.

Our short time together has already revealed that Blake's a deep thinker, carefully weighing every angle before he speaks. I'm sure that stems from keeping his secrets locked down tight, and I wonder briefly if that means I'm the reason for his current state. If he's having second thoughts about what it means to be with me. Then he blinks me into focus as he registers my presence, and he smiles so big I'm damn near blinded by his white teeth.

Whatever had him preoccupied seconds ago is gone—it straight up vanishes—as he leaps up from the couch and closes the distance between us, wrapping his arms around my shoulders and pulling me firmly against his chest. *No second thoughts, then.*

"Damn I'm glad you're back." His voice is raspy against my ear. "Do you need help unpacking?"

"Later." I reach behind his head and pull him to me, crushing our lips together. The combination of soft lips and rough stubble brush against me. The sensation has my cock stirring, and after several days apart it's eager for his touch. I drag my hand down his chest, over his flat stomach, until I find the button on his shorts. "It's been too long," I groan, tugging it open.

"Holy hell." Blake's head falls back as I take him in my fist, already hard as granite for me. "I guess you missed me, too?"

It's on the tip of my tongue to play coy, to say something like I missed his dick, so I don't come on too strong. The words don't come, though. Instead, I pull my rigid cock out and line it up with his, stroking both of us together. "What do you think?" I rasp.

"I think there's nothing hotter than feeling your dick rub against mine." Blake puts just enough distance between our chests that he can watch my hand move. "Bedroom. Now," he growls.

"Later. This feels too good to stop."

Blake groans but makes no attempt to move. Trapped in my fist, he rocks his hips slightly, chasing the friction between us. It's mind blowing.

If I'm being honest, a hard dick is one of my favorite things to feel next to my own. Not that I don't enjoy a wet mouth, a warm pussy, or a tight ass. They all feel fucking incredible. But they're all soft in their own way, and sometimes you just want the unyielding pressure of a firm cock pressing against yours.

Standing in the living room, shorts pooled around our ankles, I stroke and squeeze and fondle us both, coaxing him to the brink. Each time I feel him start to lurch in my fist, I let go and reach for his balls, massaging them until his release is out of reach. Then I start all over again, teasing him to the point of no return and backing off before he falls over it.

"Jace, please," he groans after I've edged him for the third time. The desperation in his tone has me nearly ready to burst, and I work him until we both explode. Our cum mixes together as it drips over my fist. *Best homecoming ever.*

Blake staggers over to the couch and collapses onto the cushions, chest heaving underneath the thin fabric of his shirt. I strip mine off to clean up and pull up my boxers before flopping down next to him.

"If that's what happens when you come home from a trip, I'm less opposed to Axel dragging you away for work." Blake lifts his head up just long enough for his eyes to roam over me then lets it fall limp against the cushion.

"I'm not sure how much work I'll have with him now that he's got this new training venture." I run a hand through my hair to brush the sweaty strands off my forehead. "We haven't talked specifics about his future plans, although my guess is he'll retire from the competition circuit sooner rather than later, which probably means less travel for me. Speaking of work, how's the new boss."

Blake opens his mouth and shuts it, opens it again, and blows out a frustrated breath. "She's... cool."

"She? You didn't tell me it was a woman."

"I didn't know that myself until she was here. And that's not the only surprise." He lifts his head, eyes darting nervously to mine as he licks his lips.

The panicky feeling I had earlier comes back with a vengeance, and I struggle to keep my voice level. "What?"

"Turns out I already knew her. We..." He drops his gaze to his lap, which like mine is only covered by the thin fabric of his boxers.

"You fucked," I sigh, closing my eyes.

"Yeah." His fingers tug at the material hugging his thigh.

"Did you again?" I'm surprised at how calm I sound when my heart feels like it's going to beat out of my chest. *What's the right response here?* Normally, I wouldn't care if a guy took a detour with a girl, but normally, I don't feel a connection to the guys I fuck. I don't think I like the idea of Blake being with anyone but me, even a woman, especially without telling me. Then again, I'm the one who specified only other men were off limits. Maybe I don't have a right to respond at all?

"No. I didn't sleep with her." Blake says evenly. Too evenly.

"You wanted to, though."

"I told you I could be monogamous. I was. *I am.*" It's not an admission, but he's not disagreeing with me, either. He did want to sleep with her, and I can't be upset about that because I'm the one who left that door open. I'm the one who said we shouldn't sleep with other *men*, mainly because I wanted the option to sleep with women if desire struck.

Monogamy doesn't scare me—if I'm with Blake, I'm with him—but ignoring part of who I am... that does.

I'm not and never will be gay. I'm not and never will be straight. I guess that's why—in my mind—I could have a monogamous relationship and still satisfy my other needs. Like, I could be committed to Blake and only Blake as far as men go, but still sleep with other women. Or I could date a man and a woman, like this couple I met a few years back who did just that. Until a few minutes ago, either scenario made perfect sense. Now that Blake's bumped into a former lover, one he clearly still has an interest in, I'm re-thinking that.

Am I being selfish? Probably. It just never occurred to me that I wouldn't want to share him, even with another woman. But if I think I might want a woman again one day, it's not fair of me to keep him from this one. *Shit.* People say relationships are complicated, but I thought it'd take longer to get to the complicated part.

Twisting so I can see him, I brace an elbow on the back of the couch. "So, we said we'd see how things go with us... How do you want them to go?"

The crease in his brow tells me he's worried, and despite feeling confused, I reach for his hand.

"I want them to get going. I don't want to screw things up because my former lover suddenly lives here."

"Lover, or someone you could love?" I ask softly.

He gnaws the inside of his lip with his teeth before speaking. "Honestly, I think it could go either way. She's pretty cool. Hot. The kind of girl I'd want to get serious with. She's also now my boss, and even if she's the kind of girl I *could* love, I'm with you." He finally looks me in the eye, and even though I know this girl showing up has him rattled, the way he holds my gaze tells me he's serious about us.

I don't have the words to tell him how much I appreciate his honesty. All I know is, I owe him the same in return, even if it takes us down a path I'm not sure I want to follow. "I know you're with me, but I don't know if that means you can't be with her."

My comment lingers in the air a beat before Blake finally speaks. "What are you saying?"

"For guys like us, being *together* might look different. Maybe it means no other guys but girls are fair game?"

Blake sucks in a mouthful of air. "Is that what you want?"

"Not at the moment, no." I brush my thumb over the back of his hand. "But if a girl I've been with suddenly appeared in front of me, one I really liked, I don't know how I'd feel. I never really operated under the assumption that I'd have to choose between people I like."

"You never wanted a relationship?" His tone isn't defensive, just curious.

"I never thought a relationship had to fit a certain definition, like only involving two people."

"You're telling me I should date both of you?" His brows disappear underneath his disheveled hair.

"I'm saying I understand that you might feel pulled toward two different people. I'll respect it if you want to see this woman, too."

Exhaling heavily, Blake watches my finger, which is still moving slowly over his hand. "Look, I won't deny that seeing her threw me, especially since I think I'd want something with her under different circumstances. But I *have* always assumed relationships are between two people, and everything about you and I feels right. I don't want it to end before it starts, and I can't think of a better way to screw this up than to try to date someone else while I'm with you."

Selfishly, that's what I wanted him to say. I need him to be positive though, considering he's a big part of the reason I'm going to try living in this town. The most important part. "A girl you could love might solve your coming out of the closet problem. It'd make things a lot easier for you."

Blake's nostrils flare as he pins me with a determined frown. "I don't want easy, I want real, whatever that looks like. And this," he draws a line between the two of us with his free hand, "feels real. I can't explain why that is when it happened so fast..."

"It is real," I growl, yanking him to me so I can press my lips to his. "That's the only explanation. Now, get dressed and help me move into my new bedroom."

Taking charge lets me mask the relief I feel over not having to share Blake with anyone else, and as an added bonus he seems to like it. Yet hours later, as we drift off, I can't help wondering if we're destined to fail.

I don't doubt Blake when he says he's focused on the two of us. He clearly believes it. I just wonder if he'll feel the same after working next to this woman day after day, especially when his life really would be easier if he chose her over me.

Chapter 14

Becca

Despite the awkward first day, where I basically propositioned my employee, Blake and I quickly fall into a comfortable rhythm. I still drool over him when he's not looking of course, but after just a few days, we've got a friendly rapport that makes working side-by-side easy.

As a lifelong resident of Katah Vista, he knows *everyone*, and he makes sure they all know me. He doesn't just introduce me either, he talks up the work I did in Utah, and praises my plans for the park here. And he defers to me without any undertone or sour expression, which has everyone on the team treating me with respect. I'd have earned that on my own—by doing good work—but his example made things harmonious from day one. Even though I didn't want or need him to make things easier for me, it's nice to focus on making progress instead of proving myself.

No matter how much everyone professes to be okay working for me, I'm still a woman in a male dominated field, so there's a certain amount of skepticism that comes with the territory. I'm so used to it, I can't even say it sucks anymore—it just *is*. Having Blake to stop the bullshit before it starts means the whole crew falls into sync faster, and since we want to have something ready to ride by the end of the summer season, I can't complain. Plus, the guy makes me laugh on the regular, and who doesn't like to have fun while they work?

Blake has an endless amount of "local lore" to share, mostly harmless in nature, like how his favorite bar, The Underground, used to be off-limits because the older men in town had claimed it as their own, and didn't want young "riff raff" in their space. That changed when his friend Dex bought the place. According to him, some of the gentlemen still grumble about it. My favorite tale, though, is about a local outlaw.

I guess it wasn't uncommon in the old days for people to lay low here, since the town is so remote, and most people don't ask too many questions. Draft dodgers were common, but one guy, known only as Phil, was arrested for drug trafficking after living here nearly thirty years. It later came out that Phil wasn't his real name, but no one had any reason not to believe the guy who volunteered at the local school, theater, and fire department. It came as quite the shock when the FBI swooped in to snatch him up.

Blake's animated storytelling and easygoing personality make the time pass quickly, which I appreciate. Unfortunately, they also make him even more attractive to me. I do my best to ignore that and just appreciate being in the outdoors, doing what I love. Although, most days I can't help resenting the boundaries he's set. I won't ignore them, but internally I struggle to keep things platonic, and I'm constantly having to remind myself not to daydream about the night we shared.

It's harder than it should be, and as I'm walking back to my office it occurs to me that my daydreams are making me see things, because there's no way the only other guy I've been with since my breakup with Brian just passed in front of me carrying a stack of boxes.

Get a grip, Becca. I shake my head to clear it. It's a halfhearted effort, because that's another nice image. We may have only had the one night, but I'd confessed to just coming out of a relationship, and Jace had taken extra care to make me feel treasured, as if he could sense I needed that reassurance from a man. I wasn't foolish enough to think our time together was as special for him as it was me. It was a hookup plain and simple, but I loved that he didn't treat me as one of many.

For me it wasn't just sex, but something that restored my confidence and sense of self-worth. And yes, mind-blowing orgasms. Can't forget those. As a result, a tiny part of my heart has belonged to him ever since. I always hoped I'd see him again—he's friends with my old boss Jackson—but his job as a videographer for some pro biker keeps him on the road non-stop.

I heard he'd been to visit Jackson a few weeks back, but I'd been visiting my sister and missed him. That's when I met Blake, the other hookup who treated me as more than just a one-night stand. That must be why I'm manifesting Jace now. I can't have what I want with Blake so I'm substituting Jace in the lead role of that daydream. It seems plausible, until I realize I'm still staring at the doorway he seemed to disappear into, and he comes walking out of it.

Hot damn, he looks good. Tall and lean, with muscled calves flexing as he walks, he looks just as dark and brooding from afar as I remember him, though I know all too well his feelings run deep under that stoic exterior. It's one of the things that draws me to him, the knowledge that the sexy outer shell hides a gentle soul. The same way Blake's does. Apparently, that's my type, and somehow the two men who fit that criteria are here. In my new hometown.

I can tell the moment Jace sees me, pausing mid-stride as if he's trying to reconcile what he sees. Despite having a few minutes head start, I feel the same way, barely finding the strength to lift the hand hanging limply at my side in a tiny wave. That breaks him out of his stupor, and he stalks forward, closing the distance between us.

"Becca?" He cocks his head to the side, voice filled with disbelief.

"Hi." I cringe as the word squeaks from my mouth.

"I looked for you when I passed through Utah this summer. You weren't at the resort, but Jackson didn't make it sound like you'd left." Jace's eyes roam over me as if he still doesn't trust that they're seeing things correctly.

"I heard. I was visiting my sister." My hand waves in the general direction of her house in Arizona, as if that would mean anything to him. *First, Blake and now Jace? Why am I suddenly a disaster around guys I'm drawn to?*

"What are you doing here?" The hint of a smile tugs at the corner of his lip, and my stomach flutters.

"I live here now. Just moved in the other day. I'm in charge of building the new bike park. They want to create something similar to what we created in Utah, and since I helped Jackson design that one, he recommended me for the job." *Stop rambling.*

Jace looks me up and down before wiping a hand down his face. "You're Bec?"

The nickname brings a smile to my face. "Only Jackson calls me that."

He shakes his head back and forth with a bewildered laugh. "All these years, Jackson raved about his assistant, Bec. I never realized it was you. Why didn't you say something before?"

I feel my cheeks turning as pink as my hair as I look anywhere but his eyes. "We sort of... didn't talk much about work that night."

"I told you what I did." He folds his arms in front of his chest and arches a thick brow.

"Only because I saw all the camera gear in your hotel room. And when I asked about it all you said was you make highlight videos of some pro motocross rider, and you were only in town for the night before you had to go to the next location. I don't know who you film or how you got into that, or how you know Jackson come to think of it."

A playful grin spreads across his face. "Yeah, sounds about right. I wouldn't have wanted to spend our only night together talking about work."

"So, why are *you* here? Is this a location for one of your shoots?"

"It was last month. Axel, the guy I film, decided to stay."

"And open a restaurant?" I look around his shoulder to the doorway he came from, which reads 'Murphy's on the Mountain,' in the same type as the Murphy's I went to on Main Street a few days ago with Blake.

He jerks a thumb over his shoulder. "That's his girlfriend's place. They roped me into moving a few boxes."

"Lennon? That's your boss's girlfriend?"

"You know Lennon?" His eyes grow wide.

"I met her the other day."

He gives me a warm smile that I feel down to my toes. "In a town this small I shouldn't be surprised you met his girl already."

"You still haven't said why you're here. Just visiting, or..." I gnaw the inside of my cheek as I wait for him to answer, mainly so I don't flash him an eager grin. Although I'm excited to see him, that seems like the wrong response given I was just daydreaming about another guy. *Seriously though, how is it possible I run into both of them in the same town?*

Jace rubs a hand over the back of his neck. "I guess I'm sort of a resident now, too. Axel's got some stuff going on here he wants me to be a part of, so I'm checking it out."

"The two of you live together then? Where?" My words spill out too fast to be confused with polite small talk, but I can't help it. The idea of having another familiar face around, one that I always hoped I'd see again, has me on overdrive.

"Actually, he lives with Lennon. I'm..."

"Hey, Boss." I spin to find Blake jogging up with an almost wary look on his face, and I wonder briefly if he ran into a problem with the section of trail we're working on today. "I see you met my roommate."

Roommate? My fears about a work problem dissolve as I swing my head back to Jace, who's wearing an expression to match Blake's. I have the terrifying sense they know something I don't, which can only mean one thing. *They know I've slept with both of them.*

My gaze darts between the two men standing before me, as my palms start to sweat. *How? Why?*

I've never been so mortified. Twice in my life I've had a one-night stand, and now they're both standing before me, seemingly aware of the *connection* between us. Even though I'm not a promiscuous girl, there's no way they'd believe that considering they both shared my bed the day we met.

Oh God, if they know *that* what else do they know? Did they talk about our encounters? Swap stories? Neither struck me as the type to talk about their sexscapades, though that was easier to believe when I thought they were strangers to each other. And dammit, even knowing they might have violated my privacy doesn't erase the significance of my time with either of them.

Both Blake and Jace played a role in restoring my confidence, making me feel worthy. I can't regret that no matter the awkwardness of seeing them both together. I just wish they didn't have a reason to assume they were merely hookups for me when the reality is so much more intense. What other conclusion can they draw under these circumstances, though?

The giddy excitement coursing through me just moments ago evaporates, leaving me with a hollow cavity in my chest, and it takes all my willpower to breathe without hyperventilating. *WTF?*

"I uh... yeah, we met." I trap my lips between my teeth as I glance at each of them in turn, wondering how I'm supposed to face either of them again. *Can the ground reach up and swallow me whole, or does that only happen in cartoons?*

Chapter 15

Blake

Something about the way Becca's eyes fly between us in a daze is off. I have a sinking suspicion I know why that is, but this isn't the time or place, so I force my expression to remain blank and pretend nothing weird is going on.

"I've been meaning to introduce you two. Jace is a videographer, and when we get something tangible to show off I figure he can film some nice promos for the new park." I'm talking out of my ass, though it does the trick, and she snaps out of her trance.

"Yeah." She blinks in rapid succession as her mind catches up to her mouth. "That's a great idea. If it's okay with you." She angles her head and looks hesitantly at Jace, a mixture of longing and...sadness in the eyes that linger too long on my boyfriend.

"I'd love to. Blake can take me up to scout some good shots once you get further along."

"Sure." I nod in agreement. "So hey, what brings you up here today? I figured you'd be at Axel's?" I'm reaching, but in the back of my mind I'm hoping the more I talk the less awkward this gets.

Jace jerks his head toward the restaurant behind him, finally loosening up. "Axel roped me into helping move some stuff for Lennon.

This was my last trip and I've got my truck. I can give you a lift home if you're done for the day."

I glace toward Becca and lift my brows. "Anything else you need, Boss?"

"No," she blurts way too fast, which sets off a sharp pang in my chest. I have the sudden urge to reach for her, offer some type of reassurance for whatever it is she's feeling, but I have a strong suspicion that things between the three of us are more complicated than my history with Becca, which means I can't do anything before talking to Jace.

"Okay, see you tomorrow, then." I give her the warmest smile I can as Jace seems to do the same, then we both make our way to the parking lot in silence. It's the first time either of us have been at a loss for words, which only confirms my initial thoughts.

Jace starts the engine before I find the courage to admit them. "When did you sleep with Becca?"

He runs a hand through his hair before glancing in the rearview mirror and backing out. "About a year ago," he answers as he shifts the truck into drive. "I met her at the resort when I was playing around on the bike park. We clicked."

I expected that, and while it doesn't make me angry, it does have me confused. "So, when I said my new boss was a girl and I'd hooked up with her you had no idea it was Becca? She was Jackson's assistant for God's sake."

"I'm just as shocked by this as you." His wide brown eyes meet mine briefly before darting back to the road. "Jackson always talked about Bec, not Becca. I never realized it was a nickname until she told me that a few minutes ago."

My head bobs absently as his words sink in. I hate to admit it, but that's just as plausible as me not realizing Jackson's assistant was a woman, since no one specifically mentioned it. It's one hell of a coincidence, both of us sleeping with the same woman and not connecting the dots before now. Though it pales in comparison to the real issue. "You said you clicked. What does that mean?"

Jace's grip tightens on the steering wheel, giving me my answer.

"It was more than just sex. Shit," I answer for him. My head falls against the headrest as the magnitude of this sinks in.

"What makes you say that?" He sends a nervous glance my way as he turns out of the resort.

"The way she was looking at you. The woman could barely look away. Like you're important to her."

He shakes his head without taking his eyes off the road. "That's the look she was giving you."

My heartbeat accelerates with those words, though it feels wrong to enjoy them sitting next to my boyfriend, so I deflect. "You were staring at her the same way," I retort, "like nothing else existed. You want her."

"I... Shit." He slaps the steering wheel with the palm of his hand. "I did. Maybe I still do? I don't know... I was happy to see her," he adds.

"Is she a former lover, or someone you could love?" I ask softy. I don't need him to answer to confirm which she is, but if we have any hope of staying together, I need to know he'll be honest about this.

Jace flexes his hand on the wheel. "I've been with my fair share of women over the years, and she's the only one I've thought about after..." He swallows audibly and tenses his jaw. "I don't know if that means I could love her. I just know she's special somehow."

"I get it," I sigh. "There's something about her..."

"She's been hurt before," he cuts me off. "I kind of want to protect her, only..."

"Only she's not weak, and you admire that," I finish the thought that might as well have been my own.

A nostalgic smile tugs at the corner of Jace's lip. "Yeah. Before her, I didn't know a person could be fragile and strong at the same time."

"Before her I didn't know just talking could be such a turn on. Or pink hair."

"It looks amazing on her doesn't it." Jace relaxes back into the driver's seat, his earlier stiffness gone.

"I'm sorta partial to the bike shorts she wears." I close my eyes, picturing the way her sleek calves poke out from those shorts as she walks. "Damn, she looks good in those."

"She's sexy as hell on a bike."

"And in bed." *Yeah, I went there, only because it's true.*

"Fuck!" Jace slaps the wheel again. "This is either gonna make things real simple or real complicated."

"How could they possibly be simple?" I snort.

I see Jace shrug from the corner of my eye. "The three of us already like each other."

"The key word there is *three*. As in more than two." I pin him with a look that says *do the math.*

"You and I are bi. If we date a woman together it means we don't have to ignore part of who we are." His words come out so nonchalantly, you'd almost think they were no big deal, but for me it's a very big deal. I struggled most of my life to figure out if I preferred men or women, and even when I finally realized I didn't have to pick, I never considered that I could have *both* at the same time. Not permanently, not even temporarily. That's not how relationships work, right? He can't be suggesting that. Can he?

"Let me get this straight, are you implying we share a woman? That we share each other? Isn't that like cheating?" I rub my forehead to stave off the tension behind my eyes.

"Not if we all agree to it."

"Hold up." I lift my hand like a stop sign. "Why are we having this conversation? Just yesterday we agreed to focus on *us*, trying to make that work."

"And today we know we both have a thing for the same woman." He pulls into the driveway and parks the car, turning to look at me fully for the first time all afternoon. "Plus, she has a thing for us."

"*Had* a thing for us. Separately. We have no idea if she'd like us together. Or be okay with us as partners." I climb out of the cab and head toward the front door with Jace on my heels.

"So, we invite her over and ask." He shuts the door behind us as we step inside.

"Ask her what exactly?" I spin to face him. "To be the third wheel? Our fuck buddy? Even if I was into that idea, I like her too much to treat her that way."

"Whoa." He holds his hands up in surrender. "First off, I'm not suggesting we treat her like some toy for our amusement, although threesomes are seriously hot. Just saying. Second." He reaches for the waistband of my shorts and tugs me to him so he can rest his hands on my hips. "Can you honesty tell me you aren't a little torn? I mean, I know you want to be with me, and you'd be with only me if I asked you to. But the feelings you have for her will still be there, right? And you'll feel guilty about putting her aside."

I must do something to confirm he's right because the next thing I know his fingertips are under my chin, forcing me to look into the depths of his soulful brown eyes. "You think I don't feel the same way?

I want *you*, but that doesn't mean I can switch off what I feel for her any more than you can. And that's okay."

"How is that okay? How is it fair to either of you if I'm not committed to one of you?"

Jace cups the side of my face and gives me a gentle kiss. "Think of it like this. I know how amazing you are, and how amazing she is. How could I ignore one of you in favor of the other?"

That's harder to answer than I expect.

It's still hard for me to wrap my brain around, but what Jace says makes a certain amount of sense. I really like Jace, and I made a commitment to him because he was here first. Had Becca been first to arrive, I could just as easily have made that commitment to her, and the idea that I'd have missed being with Jace because of something like an arbitrary move-in date doesn't sit well. But that's what I'm doing with Becca, so maybe I'm still missing out. Maybe we all are.

"For argument's sake, let's say I agree to this. What then?"

"Well," he bites his lip thoughtfully, "I think you might be right about the whole *being into us separately* thing, so while I think she's still interested, we might have to ease into the three of us actually dating."

"And how the hell do we do that?"

"Sex."

"You literally just said we wouldn't do that to her." I take a step back and cross my arms, giving him a hard stare.

"Calm down a second, okay? Think about it." Jace runs a hand through his hair. "Even though we both think our time with Becca was about more than sex, that's how it started, right?" He waits for my nod to continue, which I grudgingly give him. "Then that's how we pick it back up. We tell her neither of us want that to be our only night with her, but we don't want to put her in a position where she has to choose between us, so we're willing to share if she is."

"That sounds an awful lot like fuck buddies." I rub my temples with a heavy sigh.

"It's exactly how we ended up together." Jace arches a thick brow in my direction as he draws a line between the two of us. "We start with sex and see where it goes, just like you and I have. Since she still seems to be into both of us, I think it'll naturally evolve into more."

"Speaking of us, what do we tell her? She'll really feel like a third wheel if we ask her to join *our* bed."

"Maybe we leave out the *us* part until she gets comfortable with the three of us together."

"You mean lie?" I pull my brows together.

"I mean do exactly what we're already doing by keeping things between us behind closed doors." He shoots me a pointed look.

Fuck, he's got me there.

I pace back and forth in the small entry, my nerves making me jittery. "You seriously think this could work? As in the three of us could be a... I don't even know what to call it."

"A throuple. And yeah, I think it could. More and more people like us are doing it."

"You're really not bullshitting me about this?" Up until this point I was half convinced he was making this up. I mean, *three people*? That's not normal. Intriguing, sure. But in a fantasy sort of way. Only, he's got too many solutions for this to be strictly fantasy.

Jace takes my hand and leads me to the couch, pulling me down so I'm between his legs with my back to him. "A few years ago, I hooked up with a husband and wife. They had a good thing going, but he was bi, and she encouraged it. They wanted another man in their life, and for a night I was that man. At the time, I wasn't in a place to consider a relationship, but ever since then, I've been sort of fascinated by the idea that I could have the same thing one day, with the right people. What's more right than three people who already have a connection?" His hands roam up my back and over my shoulders, kneading at the gathering knots. "So, what do you think?"

Chapter 16

Jace

Fuck, Blake's tense. I get it, sort of.

Never in my wildest dreams could I have predicted I'd wake up with a new boyfriend and end the day talking about adding a girlfriend to the mix. But that's the thing, having a boyfriend *and* a girlfriend *is* my wildest dream, so it's not freaking me out.

If I hadn't bumped into that couple who wanted to find a third person, I might not be as open to the idea of trying to bring Becca into this. Their desire opened my eyes, and made the whole thing seem less taboo. I didn't necessarily think it would be realistic, which is why it became a dream. With Blake and Becca, though, it feels like it could be a reality.

I lean forward, placing tiny kisses on the side of Blake's neck as I massage his shoulders. "Talk to me," I whisper.

His torso rises as he inhales deeply, then deflates as he lets the breath out. "I understand what you're saying about not wanting to choose between two equally incredible people. I can get on board with that to a degree. What I don't get is how to make sure one of the three doesn't feel left out. I mean, what if something happens between Becca and

I while you're traveling or something? You wouldn't be upset about that?"

"Honestly, the *idea* of you two together is a huge turn on for me. I'd enjoy any combination between the three of us, including one-on-one time I may or may not be part of." I feel some of the stiffness leave his body as I continue working his muscles.

"So, the three of us—as a throuple—that's not just having fun, that's a long-term thing?" He glances back to meet my gaze, brow furrowed as he considers my words.

"I think it could be. If that's what we all want."

"Even here? It's not an overly conservative town, but as far as I know there isn't even another gay couple here, let alone anyone bi. Two is...well it seems like it'd be an easier thing for people to accept than three."

"Is that you talking, or the town? Look." I clasp his chin in my fingers and nudge it so he's looking at me over his shoulder. "I know you never envisioned being with two people at the same time, and if you don't want that I won't force it. But a part of you is obviously curious, all I'm asking is for you to consider it."

Blake's eyes roam over my face, searching, but my gaze doesn't waver. I want to pursue the three of us as much as I wanted to pursue filming, but not at the expense of what I have with Blake. If he's out, so am I. When he shoots me a tentative smile, I know he must see the truth of that in my face.

"So...three. At a time. How does that work exactly?"

My tongue darts out to swipe over my lower lip. "Close your eyes." Blake exhales deeply as his eyelids drift shut. "Lean back." My hand falls to his chest, pulling his back against my front as I recline into the couch.

His weight settles against me like a thick blanket, familiar and comforting. How that's possible in such a short span of time, I can't say. I just know that it feels right to have him pressed against me, with our breaths in sync.

My fingers dip beneath his shirt to wander over his pecs, along the slim lines of his stomach. Where I'm sinewy, Blake is trim without being cut, and my hands glide effortlessly over his smooth skin, mapping the dips and planes of his body as he relaxes into my touch.

Blake's head rests against my shoulder, giving me a clear view down his body, and the bulge of the fabric between his legs. I drag my fingers over his warm skin to the waistband of his shorts. With a quick flick, I have them undone and Blake lifts his hips cooperatively so I can pull them down and free his dick. It springs up, already stiff enough to stand at attention, and mine starts to harden in response.

Fishing my wallet from my pocket, I grab the packet of lube I keep stashed there and squeeze a few drops onto my palm. Then I wrap my right hand around the base of his cock and drag my fist up his length, repeating the motion with my left.

A contented sigh passes through his lips as I stroke him from root to tip, giving the head a firm squeeze with each pass. "Picture two hands running up your length. One big and warm, one small and cool. Both of them tugging and pulling, teasing your slit." I swipe my thumb over the sensitive skin at the tip, smiling to myself when I hear the sharp intake of breath.

"Or one set working your dick while the other plays with your balls." My hand falls between his legs to roll them around in my left hand as the right glides up and down his length.

"You're doing that now with only two hands," he says through gritted teeth.

"Imagine it was four. You'd have fingers teasing your cock, your balls, *and* your ass, all at the same time." I play with the skin underneath his balls, and the subtle suggestion has him groaning in desire.

Blake's hips strain forward, a silent plea for more pressure, more speed... *just more*, though I'm content with the slow pace. I like the feeling of his firm dick in my fist, the smooth skin of his balls on my fingers. And I really like the way his ass brushes over my cock as he thrusts and swivels, chasing my hand. Mostly though, I want to give him what he hasn't had much of before... *foreplay*.

Given what I know about his history with guys, Blake's had more rushed encounters than passionate ones, and while those may come with a dose of adrenaline due to the risk of getting caught, there's something to be said about building up the anticipation. Taking him to the brink and backing off, talking through what I'm doing, drawing out my movements, all of it adds up to a killer release, and I'm going to do my best to give him one. *Eventually*.

"Don't forget about mouths." I nibble on the soft spot below his ear as I relax my grip. "One sucking on your balls while the other tongues your dick. Or both of them licking up and down your shaft, fighting over which gets to take you down their throat."

"Jesus," he gasps, arching into my hand.

Blake's cock is downright inflexible in my fist, and my own is as hard as a lead pipe, spearing into his back. The need to free it, to sink it into Blake's perfect ass, is all consuming. But I grit through the discomfort to make this epic for him.

"Tongues swiping together around the tip of your dick while four sets of fingers squeeze and pull and tug...and penetrate." I swipe the tip of my finger over his hole and am rewarded with a startled gasp that turns into a needy moan. It's so fucking sexy I can't stop myself from reacting, spearing upward in search of more friction. That earns me another moan. Despite really, *really* enjoying the way he feels in my hand, I'm helpless to ignore what my body demands.

I reach between us to push down my shorts and pull out my own throbbing dick, the movement drawing Blake's attention to where my wallet sits on the cushion beside me. He reaches for it, pulling out a condom that he hands to me before snatching the packet of lube and squirting some on his fingers.

He works the lube between his cheeks as I wrap myself up, both of us in a rush to get the prep over with. Then he sinks onto my length, coming to a rest when I'm fully seated.

We stay like that, joined, taking shallow breaths, until our bodies adjust. It has the added benefit of taking the edge off, just a fraction, knowing I'm closer to the release I desperately want. The one we desperately need. Then he starts to move, griding his ass on my cock as I take his in my hand, stroking just as leisurely as he rocks over me.

"Now picture filling Becca like I'm filling you." I brush my fingers over his tip again as a contented sign floats out of his mouth. "Her slippery heat coating your length, making it so easy to slide in and out of her warm pussy." I squeeze him in my fist as I pull along his length. "The three of us, naked and sweaty and *connected*, moving as one as the pressure builds between us. Driving each other closer and closer to the edge."

"You kiss me over your shoulder as I drive into you," I continue, fighting to ignore the way he contracts around me as I put my fantasy to words, "which makes you pump into her. Then you kiss her as you bottom out, and I withdraw to start all over again. Kissing and thrusting and groping, hands and tongues covering all the skin they can find." My grip is firm on his dick now, my strokes faster, although I'm still not jerking him without abandon. Not yet. Once I do, it will only be seconds until this is over, and I'm not ready to let that happen.

Blake grinds down hard, his ass clenching around my dick as he strains to feel it rubbing against his prostate. The pressure nearly undoes me, and I take a shaky breath as I force down the desire to let go.

Cupping his balls with my free hand, I tug his cock as I pump deeply into him, trying to hit all his pleasure points at once. The cry that bursts from his throat is damn near inhuman, and I'm helpless to ignore it the way that makes my groin tingle. Despite my best intentions, that sound robs me of all restraint, and before I know it I'm jutting my hips up as I jerk my hand over his length as fast as my muscles will allow.

The tip of my dick slams against his prostate over and over again, sending a current of electricity from the head of my cock all the way down to my balls. My thighs quiver and my ass goes numb under the strain of my efforts to drive deeper, but the discomfort barely registers as I chase the release building in my nuts.

"Can you feel it? Can you feel how good the three of us would be together?" I pant, speeding us toward the finish. Seconds later, Blake's whole body tenses, his ass convulsing around my length as his twitches in my hand. Warm liquid spills over my knuckles as his tremors tip me over the edge, and I growl in satisfaction as my cock pulses inside him. His jaw hangs open, though no sound escapes, as if even his voice is too paralyzed with pleasure to function. That's new, but it makes my chest swell with pride.

As Blake's tremors subside, I take my hands off his junk and wrap them around his waist, pinning him to me while our breathing returns to normal. In this moment, holding him close, it's hard to justify thinking about anyone else. And yet, knowing how well I fit with Becca, and how well she fits with Blake, it seems ludicrous to think the three of us wouldn't be the perfect complement to each other.

I don't mean sexually either, although there is that. It's more the sense of belonging I feel with each of them. The way I was instantly comfortable in their presence. If she were here right now, I think I'd feel just as content as I do with just Blake.

"You really think it's a good idea to ask her to be part of this?" Blake breaks the silence. "It won't take away from what we have right now?"

I kiss the side of his neck as I get my words together. "I think we could miss out on something great if we ignore the signs."

"What signs?" He twists his head so he can see my face.

"The ones that keep happening. Seriously?" I challenge his blank stare. "I'm not even the sign guy and I'm seeing them everywhere." That's not an easy thing to admit seeing as how I like to believe I'm in charge of my life, but even I have to acknowledge there have been far too many coincidences lately. "I don't think we should ignore them."

"What signs?" he repeats, a tiny crease separating his brows as he studies me.

"Well, for starters, I bumped into you in Utah of all places, and right after that Axel has a proposition for me that means living here—here being the spare room that lets us explore this thing we have at a pace you're comfortable with." When his expression doesn't change, I continue. "Then the *one* woman we both thought we could be serious about just moved *here*. She gets the job that lets you leave the spa, *here*, in the random tiny town we're in. What are the odds of jobs and living arrangements for three separate people who like each other aligning like that? You're the sign guy, are you really not seeing what I'm seeing?"

"When you put it that way..." A smile tugs at the corner of his lip. "I guess maybe that's too big a coincidence to just ignore."

"Fuck yeah. And let's not forget you didn't just have the best orgasm of your life *imagining* what it would be like to have her with us."

"It was pretty phenomenal." The tiny smile morphs into a dopey grin.

"That's an understatement," I snort. "You lost the ability to speak. Trust me when I say the real thing would be even better."

"Yeah, but when you say the real thing, you don't mean just inviting her to bed, you mean the three of us dating each other. That's a lot more intense than just fucking." His head flops back to rest on my shoulder. *Shit, he's back to feeling confused.*

"I know you don't see what I see yet, not completely," I start, "but I think you might if you give it a try. And if I'm right, if it works between us, we'll face the questions and the confusion people have together. I'm not saying that will make it easy, but none of us will be alone."

Blake's body relaxes into mine as he sighs. Picking up my hand, he threads his fingers through mine, letting them rest on his stomach. "Okay. I trust you."

The breath I didn't realize I was holding seeps out. *Holy shit, signs are real.*

Chapter 17

Becca

The hours that normally fly by are dragging today, which I suspect is because I'm not focused on work. Instead, my mind is stuck in a loop, replaying the encounter with the two men I feel certain now know have both shared my bed.

I hope neither are the jealous, possessive type, otherwise my having slept with both of them could make living together awkward, and I wouldn't want to come between roommates.

Roommates. Gah – how awkward is that? I've only indulged in sexy times *twice* in the last year, but with those two guys living together they're bound to think they're two of many. Even though I'm not a prude, I hate the idea that they might think of me as loose. That's not a reputation I want, particularly among the two men who hold a special place in my heart for the way they made me feel during our brief time together. And don't even get me started on the fact that I'll have to face one of those men every day at work. There's literally no escape.

I want to kick and scream and cry over the fact that there are two people who meet my definition of the perfect guy right in front of me, yet neither of them is available. Yes, that makes me sound like someone who's desperate for love, and yeah—who doesn't want to find their person. But right now, I'd settle for just avoiding the same loneliness I came here to escape, and I'm not sure how to accomplish that in a love triangle.

Alright, that might be taking things too far. One night doesn't equal love—logically, I know that. Emotionally, I'm stuck on feeling a connection that went beyond friendship with two people that I still want and could never choose between. I'm not sure that makes friendship with either of them even possible.

My fresh start is looking more and more like a disaster waiting to happen instead of a golden opportunity, which really frosts my Cheerios, as my sister likes to say in front of her kids.

Backtracking the path I just covered–because I was so lost in thought I ended up merely walking instead of critiquing how the trail is coming together–I compare what's on the plans to what the crew has built.

This particular section contains several switchbacks—not the hairpin turns that will be on more challenging trails—but wider curves that will encourage riders to lean the bike and utilize the outer edge of the trail to maintain speed through the turn. That means the berms need to be several feet high, and I'm not sure they're as tall as more experienced riders would like, because the taller the berm the faster you can whip around the corner. This is a green run though, so it might work as is. I'll have to ride it to be sure, when we're a little further along.

"You want more dirt over here?" I lift my head to see Blake pointing at one of the turns in question. My stomach does little flips with the realization that he can read my thoughts just by looking at me.

"It crossed my mind." I glance back at the plans in my hand to avoid getting lost in his handsome face, and disguise the fact that my blush is not from the midday sun.

"Part of me wants to say we need more so I can ride this the way I want, but then I think about how it's technically a beginner trail, and maybe shorter berms will force me to go a little slower and not terrify people trying to learn."

It's like he's living inside my brain. "I'm having the same dilemma."

"How do we decide?"

"We ride it." I risk a quick peek in his direction, shooting my eyes back to the ground when I realize he's staring intently at me.

"So..." The long pause has me glancing up in time to see him awkwardly rub the back of his neck. "Want to grab pizza with Jace and I, tonight?"

Of all the things he could say, that's the last one I'm expecting to hear. "Why?"

"You're new in town—probably haven't met many people yet—and you once saved me from being the lonely guy at the bar. I'm trying to return the favor."

"That was... Things are... Do you really think that's a good idea?" I fold my lips between my teeth and hold my breath.

"Why wouldn't it be?" He lifts his shoulder casually.

I feel my eyes roll back in my head as I exhale. "Can we not pretend you don't know? Before I met you I..."

"Slept with Jace. Yeah, of course I know. It was written all over both your faces."

"That doesn't bother you?"

"No. You're fun, you're hot, you love biking... If anyone can understand why he was drawn to you it's me, and I don't have a problem knowing you've been with him. Does it bother you that you've been with both of us?" The smile he sends me borders on mischievous, almost like he's testing me.

My stomach might be doing back flips, but I'll be damned if I tell him that. Calling on my inner flamingo, I give him an equally coy grin. "Nope. All good."

"Perfect. Then there's no reason we can't all hang out together. I'll text you my address." Blake spins away with a triumphant wink, which leaves me free to freak out minus an audience.

The guys have clearly put me in the friend zone, and seeing as how I don't really know anyone here, I'm grateful for that. But my hormones aren't on board with that label quite yet, so I have no idea how I'm going to get through tonight without letting my attraction for either of them grow deeper.

***

"Glad you made it. Come on in." Blake moves aside and holds the door open so I can enter the nondescript little bungalow the guys call home.

I ditch my flip flops in the foyer and step into the living room, twisting my head right to left to take in the space before me. It's definitely a bachelor's place—no decorations to make it feel homey, like pictures or knick knacks that have been collected over time—but it's clean. Cozy.

"We've got pepperoni or supreme, which do you like?" Jace calls from the kitchen.

"One of each." I follow the voice and make my way over to a rectangular table with two bench seats. Tiny nicks and scratches mar the dark-stained wood, though they don't scream neglect, more like well-loved. Like it's a piece that's been passed down a few generations.

Jace sets a plate and a beer in front of me with a wink as he and Blake take seats across the table. The three of us dive into the food, which I suspect is a ploy to get me to relax instead of jumping into conversation. It works, considering I'm starving.

Halfway into his second slice, Jace breaks the silence. "What do you think of town so far?"

"It's got more character than I was expecting," I say around a mouthful of cheese.

An easy smile spreads across his face. "Yeah, I'd never seen a purple building until I came here. It sounds like it should be ugly but somehow it's not."

"I know right," I agree. "And Blake introduced me to a few girls in town. They seem nice, although I haven't seen any of them since that first night. I didn't get the impression any of them were big bikers, so I'm not sure what all we'll have in common."

"Tiff's a good rider although she doesn't do it much, and Cora—who you'll meet eventually—has been out a few times with her husband," Blake says. "You should start a bike group for the girls. I bet most of them would be willing to learn, and they'd probably prefer to start on a cross-country trail than a downhill one like what we're building on the mountain."

"Ooh, I like that idea." My lingering nerves about the evening fade with the mention of biking. "I need to learn the area first. Can you guys show me some good beginner trails?"

"Yeah, Blake." Jace claps his roommate on the shoulder as he gives me a conspiratorial wink. "Can you show us some trails?"

"You don't know them?" I squint in Jace's direction.

"He only got his stuff unpacked the other day. I haven't had time to show him much yet." Blake ducks his head as he stuffs a piece of crust in his mouth. *Odd.*

My gaze darts between the two of them, confusion mounting. "The other day? I thought Jace said he got here last month?"

Jace's Adam's apple bobs as he swallows a mouthful of beer. Swiping his tongue across his upper lip—which I pretend not to be affected by—he locks eyes with mine. "I didn't have a chance to move my trailer here until just this week."

Focus, Becca. "If your trailer is here, how did you two end up as roommates?" I vaguely remember him telling me how nice that trailer is, and how much he loved having his own space.

"Trailers aren't the most comfortable place to be in the winter, and Blake offered me a room." Jace casts a quick glance in Blake's direction as he clears his throat, leading me to conclude I imagined the husky tone in his voice. "Plus, I like the company." Jace's eyes find mine again, the chocolate depths making my stomach flutter. I make a mental note not to have another beer because it's making me see things that can't exist in his gaze.

"Well, Blake's an easy guy to get along with," I respond lamely.

"He is." Jace nods without averting his eyes. "I like living here. And I like having you here, too. I'm glad you came over tonight. We both are."

My skin was already starting to heat up under the intensity of his stare, but something about that comment has me peeking in Blake's direction to find a matching look on his face. *What is happening? Is this some kind of test to see if we really can be friends? And if it is, who are they testing? Me, or themselves?*

"I'm uh, glad to be here, too. It was nice to have company over dinner. I should probably be going though."

"What's the rush?" Jace's smooth voice wraps around me, causing tingles of electricity to erupt all over my body.

"You can stay as long as you want." Blake's soft invitation almost sounds like a plea. For a brief moment, I flash back to our night together, when he said the same thing after we devoured each other for the first time. Then it's gone, replaced by two gorgeous faces that have a spark of desire mixed in with their intent focus. *That's...wow. Okay, I'm officially seeing things.*

"Becca?" Jace prompts me when I don't respond.

"I... Sorry, is this really not weird for you guys?" I blurt. "I've slept with both of you. I'm still attracted to both of you. I don't know how to sit here and pretend that's normal."

"Why wouldn't that be normal?" Jace asks. "We're attracted to you, too." His voice is eerily steady. Unaffected by the impossibility of his words.

My eyelids flutter in rapid succession as I process his words. "I'm sorry, you're what?"

A hint of pink creeps into Blake's cheeks as he clears his throat. "We're both into you. The fact that you've been with both of us doesn't make either of us want you any less."

A rush of adrenaline floods my body. The notion that not one but *both* of these guys could still have an interest in me is a heady thought, one that relieves me from the doubt I felt when I realized the sordid little triangle we make. Though, instead of making me jittery or excited, that adrenaline paralyzes me, pinning me to my seat.

"Shit," Blake groans, shooting a nervous glance toward Jace as he runs a hand through his hair. "We're fucking this up. I told you this was a bad idea."

"Becca." Jace takes my hand in both of his. "Are we making you uncomfortable?"

"I... I" Trying to swallow despite my dry throat, my gaze darts helplessly between them. "What are you fucking up?"

Jace's warm smile is reassuring as he rubs his thumb over the back of my hand. "We're coming on too strong. I'm sorry. It's just that we know you're still interested in both of us, and...we're cool with that."

I pull my hand back reflexively. "I can't like both of you. That's... It's not... Someone would get hurt." I'm sure there are at least a dozen other arguments to be made, but this one comes to mind first.

"People get hurt when there are secrets, but we're not hiding the fact that we're both attracted to you." Jace's voice is still calm. Meanwhile, my heart is ready to beat out of my chest.

"Great, no secrets. I still can't pick between you."

"He's not asking you to pick," Blake says gently. "He's suggesting the three of us can... *be together.* Not you and I or you and him, all three."

"Three?" The word feels weird on my tongue. "Huh?"

"Don't choose between us, choose both." Jace shrugs casually, as if the solution is obvious.

"Both. As in I take turns with..." My eyes bulge as they meet Jace's serious gaze. "Together? At the same time together?"

I should probably be repulsed by that, but I'm actually intrigued. Two men at once? Who wouldn't be curious about that, and if I'm going to indulge in that particular fantasy, I prefer to do it with two men I trust, both of whom I happen to be insanely attracted to.

No, wait. It's one thing if it's just sex, but I actually *like* these guys. Blake is tender and sweet, an old soul in a young man's body. Jace is darker but no less deep, and makes me feel protected. They each have qualities that draw me to them as people, and while sex with both of them was incredible, I've never thought of myself as a *just sex* person. But they aren't talking about dating or relationships, so if those are off the table... The sex was *really* good.

Blake comes around the table to kneel before me, gently rubbing my knee. "I was skeptical at first too, and if we didn't all have this connection from before we all lived here, I probably wouldn't be open to pursuing it now. But I saw the way you looked at Jace the other day, and the way you look at me when you think I'm not paying attention. I can tell you still want both of us. And I can tell Jace wants you as much as I do. So, maybe the three of us being attracted to each other doesn't have to be a bad thing."

"The way I see it." Jace kneels next to Blake and puts his hand on my other knee. "This town is too small to avoid each other, and we'll struggle to hang out together if we pretend this attraction doesn't exist. So, let's not ignore it."

Trapping my lips between my teeth, I mull over his words. "I see your point, but like you said, this is a small town. I'm not sure I want to be known as the girl sleeping with two guys right off the bat."

"We don't want that for you, either." Blake's mouth forms a thin line as he shakes his head back and forth. "Whatever happens between the three of us stays between the three of us, especially since we work together."

"Speaking of work," I squint at Blake, "why the sudden change of heart? Aren't you still concerned about messing up our jobs?"

"I may have overreacted about that." He gives my knee a gentle squeeze. "We may not know each other very well yet, but I know you're not the kind of person to let personal things spill over into work."

"So, what do you think?" Jace asks.

My brain is screaming at me to say no, but my heart understands where they're coming from. I have a connection to each of them, and ignoring one for the other, or both, would make me just as miserable as choosing not to explore this, as unconventional as it may be. And yeah, there's maybe a little bit of *take that Brian* at play here, but only because I'm somehow desired by not one, but *two* men when he thought I wouldn't be desirable by *any*. It boosts my fragile confidence. That makes me want to explore the role of the self-assured, daring woman, and say yes.

"Okay." My voice is weaker than I intend—a sign that my brain is lagging behind my hormones at the moment—though the heated looks cast my way when I give consent quickly shuts my brain up. *Dear Lord, I'm about to be devoured.*

Despite a near ravenous look, Jace leans forward slowly, cupping the side of my face as he touches his lips briefly to mine. When he releases me, Blake mimics him, tipping my chin in his direction for a soft, chaste kiss. I have the sense that both men are waiting to see if I freak out, so I take care to keep my breathing steady, and my expression neutral. Evidently, that satisfies them.

"Come with us." Jace offers me a hand as he stands, and before I consciously decide to comply, I find myself doing as he says. Blake rises as well, taking my free hand in his, and leading us through the living room and down the hall to a bedroom. He stops only when we reach the side of the bed, guiding me to stand with my back to the mattress. With both of them facing me, Blake's hands drift to the hem of my shirt, where they pause as he looks at me with lifted brows. My head dips once, and the fabric glides over my skin as he lifts it up and over my head.

Jace's hand settles between my breasts, over the clasp on my bra, as he gives me a similar, inquisitive look. I nod my head again, and there's a soft *snap* as the hook joining the cups together comes undone. The cool air barely has time to kiss my skin before warm fingers brush the cups aside, baring my tits.

"Beautiful," Blake murmurs, his fingers grazing over a nipple as Jace's tongue swipes over his bottom lip.

"Lie back." Jace steps forward, forcing me to fall back on the bed.

Both men follow me, urging me to scoot until we're all sprawled sideways on the mattress, me on my back and them propped on their sides.

I inhale sharply and close my eyes as two sets of fingers dance up my stomach, over my breasts, down my arms—mapping the peaks and contours of my body. Goosebumps rise in their wake, as their light touch chills my skin even and heats my core, making my body tense of its own accord.

"Relax," a deep voice whispers in my ear, though before I can comply, a tongue flicks over my nipple, causing a needy whimper to pass through my lips.

"Fuck, I like that sound." Jace—I think—kneads my breast in his palm as he gives instructions. "Make her do it again."

The tongue finds my nipple once more, though this time it swirls around once, twice, before a hot, wet mouth covers me, sucking me into its depths.

Too overwhelmed for words, I moan and sigh, occasionally crying out as teeth and tongues and hands roam reverently over my body, leaving no part untouched. From sensual caresses to teasing strokes, I have never been so thoroughly explored, and with my eyes closed, I can almost let myself believe that it's not taboo. That this is perfectly normal. Until both my breasts are swallowed by needy mouths, or I feel a tongue on my nipple while a second one strokes against mine, stealing all sounds of pleasure before they can pass my lips.

If I concentrate—or try to think logically—I could probably tell who is doing what. But I don't want to think, *I want to feel*. So, I keep my eyes pressed shut and accept all the attention they're willing to give, reveling in the state of bliss they've brought me to.

Sometimes they move in sync, their movements softly seductive, other times they mix it up, one touching me worshipfully while the other is demanding. The dueling sensations push my arousal to the brink without ever letting me fall over the precipice. A persistent hum of pleasure courses through me as I hover in a suspended euphoria.

Eventually, I register cool air hitting my pussy—my pants must have come off while I was lost in the fog of bliss—and a set of fingers spreads me open. Then a warm tongue slides between my folds, the tip flicking seductively over my clit. My hips buck as horse whispers drift through the otherwise silent room.

"How wet is she?"

"Drenched."

"Does she taste as good as you remember?"

"Better. Like fucking heaven." The tongue swipes over me again, and my pelvis arches upward, wantonly straining for more.

I open my eyes in time to see Blake pulling his tongue back inside his mouth as Jace leans forward and closes his lips over my clit, sucking it leisurely into his hot, wet mouth. My hips lurch again, but Blake pins them down so Jace can keep his mouth on me, the two of them working together to fuel my desire. Then they shift so Blake is the one licking while Jace watches, rapt, as if witnessing Blake's tongue moving between my legs is just as hot as doing it himself.

Their heads are so close together it's almost hard to see who's doing what, and I'm not entirely sure they aren't both licking me at the same time. My lust-addled body doesn't much care, as long as they don't stop, though my brain—which finally seems to have come over to the dark side—wonders how close they are to kissing down there and is embarrassingly intrigued by the idea.

I'm helpless to stop the moan brought on by the image I conjured, which both men seem to take as a sign that I'm close to going over the edge.

"Still with us, Becca?" Jace kneels and pulls his shirt over his head, revealing the washboard abs I recall licking the last time we were together. *I'll never get tired of that view.*

"More." I pant, too turned on to care that I'm virtually begging.

"You'll get it. You've got us pretty worked up, too. See what eating your pretty pussy did to Blake." I follow his gaze to find Blake kneeling on the other side of me, totally naked, cock jutting up proudly from between his legs. "Look how hard he is." Jace's hand wraps around Blake's dick and gives it a firm tug, and I gasp as Blake grunts. *That was... sorta hot, actually.*

I didn't realize that's how threesomes work, although this is my first, so maybe two guys feeling each other is par for the course. They are naked together after all, so it makes a certain amount of sense, and it's cool they aren't squeamish about touching. I never expected to find it so intriguing, though. The throbbing between my legs intensifies as Jace releases Blake and issues another command.

"Take him in your mouth, Becca. Suck him off while I fuck you."

Blake scoots closer to my head as I feel Jace's cock probing my entrance. I open my mouth to take Blake as Jace pushes inside, and the three of us let out a collective groan once we're joined.

The guys make shallow thrusts at first, testing my limits I assume, which is sweet but not necessary. I'm so primed, I want all of them. *Now.* I press forward onto Blake's cock and moan around it, trying to tell him that, and by some miracle he understands.

"She's taking me deeper. I think she wants you to fuck her harder," Blake grits.

"I can do that." He props his forearms under my knees and leans forward, changing the angle, and thrusts long and deep. My resulting scream is muffled only by Blake's dick filling my mouth, which Jace apparently likes since he throws his head back and lets out a shout of his own.

"Holy shit," Blake pants. "I felt you scream on my cock—do that again and I'll come undone."

Jace seems to take that as a challenge, increasing his pace as he leans farther still, licking the tender spot between my neck and my collar bone that's fully exposed with my head turned toward Blake.

Between the two of them, I'm virtually trapped, unable to move my hips or my head. I can do little more than lie here and let them have their way with me. Before tonight, I would've expected that to feel demeaning, but the opposite is true. Being immobile prevents me from wondering what I should do, how I could please both of them at once. It takes away all of the pressure, giving me the freedom to just *feel*, and what I feel is mounting to what I assume will be the best orgasm of my life.

Each time Jace thrusts, I feel it deep inside my belly, a pinprick of bliss that grows stronger and fuller each time his tip hits my most sensitive nerves. I moan in earnest, which has Blake groaning above me as he pumps in and out of my mouth, and though his eyes are squeezed shut as if he's on the brink of losing control, he's lucid enough not to thrust too deep. I hollow my cheeks around him, hoping to give him the same pleasure they're giving me.

"Fuck, that's hot," Jace growls as his eyes dart between my mouth and the stunned bliss on Blake's face. Something about the naked arousal in Jace's expression—combined with his relentless thrusts—sends me spiraling, and the tiny sparks of pleasure erupt, and I feel my pussy convulse around Jace's cock as wave after wave of ecstasy spreads throughout my core.

"Oh fuck." Jace grunts as he bottoms out and holds still right as Blake says, "Can't stop...Gonna..."

Blake groans as he starts to pull back, and though I'd like to chase him, my body is too overcome with my own release to do it. And when he grabs his dick and gives it a firm tug, shooting his cum on my chest, and I swear it makes my pussy clench harder.

Jace is the first to recover, pulling out and flopping down next to me on the bed. Blake reaches for a shirt and wipes me down before doing the same. "Everyone good?" he croaks.

"Fan-fucking-tastic," I exhale. "Although, I thought a threesome meant you'd be in me at the same time."

"Only when you're ready for that." Blake brushes a strand of hair away from my face.

"There are endless combinations." Jace plants a soft kiss to my lips and gets up to get rid of the condom I don't remember him getting but am grateful he remembered.

"Endless?" I'm not sure if it's the marathon I just metaphorically ran or my curiosity that makes the word sound almost breathless, but it puts a sly grin on Jace's face.

"Endless," he repeats.

"In that case, maybe this time you two switch." I bite my lip as my eyes dart between them. *In for a penny, in for a pound, right?*

"Whatever you want, Becca." Blake kisses my forehead protectively. "Whatever you want."

Chapter 18

Jace

It's pushing midnight by the time Becca leaves our bed, and while we tried to insist she stay, I get why she didn't. I hate that she's gone, but it gives me the opportunity to make sure Blake is still okay with this.

"I hate the idea of her being alone right now," Blake tells the ceiling. His inability to look at me is a sign that he's still coming to terms with it all, despite the fact I know he enjoyed it. I imagine she's going through something similar, but I've seen Becca fall down and get up after wrecking on the bike *and* after a bad breakup, so I know she can handle this.

"We gave her a lot to process, tonight. Sometimes people want a little space for that."

"If she was okay with everything, why would she need to process it?" His fingers stroke idly over his bare chest.

I roll to face him, propping my head on my hand. "You're processing it."

His hand stills as he exhales heavily. "Yeah, I guess I am. Do you think it went too far? We weren't exactly gentle."

"I'm pretty sure she didn't want gentle. And besides," I lay my hand on his, "if we want to ease her into the idea of being in an actual relationship with us, we should avoid giving her the impression this is anything but three people having a good time. Being gentle says the opposite."

His Adam's apple bobs as he swallows. "That makes this feel cheap and dirty."

I open my mouth to object and can't find the words to do it. It makes me sick to think Becca might feel that way about what we did, but the idea of pushing her away by asking for more than she's ready to give makes me sicker.

We only had the one night together, but I've thought about her dozens of times since then. How she's both sweet yet not a pushover, innocent while still adventurous. I admire how she's willing to push beyond her comfort zone, but only for her own validation, no one else's. I've never met another woman like her, and I know the same is true for Blake. Those are big feelings to reveal in such a short time, and at the risk of sounding like a total dick, I'm not sure we should be confessing that just yet.

Taking my hand off Blake's, I rub it over my face. "I'm all for going about this differently if you have another idea. I just don't want to scare her off by getting too serious, too fast. Casual seems like a good way to get things started, and unless I'm imagining things, I think she enjoyed it. I think we all did.

"It did go better than I expected. Especially after you grabbed my cock. Why'd you do that, anyway?" He finally looks at me, brows drawn in confusion.

"You were so hard. I didn't think, I just reacted. I swear she licked her lips when she saw it, though." That little slip damn near gave me a heart attack once I realized what I'd done, and I dropped Blake's cock like a hot potato, hoping Becca didn't see me holding it. When I realized she had—and that she seemed to like it—let's just say it made the fantasy that much closer to a reality in my mind.

"You think we're that lucky? That she'd be cool with us being bi?" Blake's voice holds the same tinge of hope I feel.

"Does she strike you as the type to have a problem with it?" I trace my index finger up and down his arm, and though it's meant to be reassuring instead of sexual, it causes him to inhale sharply.

"No." It's barely a whisper. "But maybe knowing two people are bi and seeing it up close are different."

"Maybe," I agree. "Either way, it's only been one night, and while I don't get the sense she'd have a problem with us, it's still probably too soon to spring that on her."

"We should tell her before anyone else. She deserves that." Blake pops his jaw as he focuses his gaze on the ceiling again. It takes all my willpower not to smile. His protective instincts are cute.

"We will. Although," I pause until he faces me again, "Axel knows."

"What?" His eyes grow wide with alarm.

I hold my hand up in surrender, hoping to stop him from jumping to conclusions. "I didn't tell him, but he knows me well enough to guess why I moved in here. Don't worry, he won't say anything until you're ready." My hand falls back to the mattress, tracing a path up and down his arm. "Neither will I. In the closet or out, Becca or no Becca, nothing changes with us."

His body seems to sink further into the bed as the tension he was trying to hide subsides. Once again, I'm grateful to have this time with just Blake to reassure him things will be okay. Though I hated to see Becca leave as much as he did, Blake has a lifetime of confusion he's grappling with while she probably only has a night's worth. She's strong enough to get through this on her own. Blake isn't, and her absence gives him the chance to process what he's feeling instead of burying it in an attempt to comfort her.

Scooting closer, I nudge him to his side and press against him, draping my arm over his waist. "Let's stop trying to solve everything after one night. We'll figure it out as we go, right?" I repeat the mantra we've been living by since we first decided to give this thing a shot.

"Right." He relaxes into me, drifting to sleep while I hold him tight. Just yesterday, this was all I wanted, and if this is all I can have it'll still be a good life. I can't help wanting a great one, though.

***

The next morning, Blake is his usual laid-back self, and I send him off to work feeling confident that he's on board with living in the moment instead of stressing about the 'what ifs.' At least, I hope he is, because I have to concentrate on my own 'what ifs.'

I told Axel I'd help him out with his training camp idea, but I'm not sure that's the best career move for me. First off, only part of the job would involve filming. Second, it's a job, and I'm not sure I want one of those. Not when I could have my own gig.

Talking to Blake and Becca about the trails we want to explore, I realized there's probably a ton of terrain that'd be great for filming, and guys who merely pass through here—like I did last month—don't really know where that terrain is. If I live here, and have the opportunity to fully explore the place, *I'll* be the guy who knows where the best spots are, and I could be the local expert. Whether that means consulting with other film crews or doing the filming myself, I could build something that keeps me outside instead of behind a desk. And the best part is, I could do that year-round, because snowsports have just as much need for video as bike sports.

I have a lot of thinking to do before I move forward with something like that, but ever since the idea popped into my mind at dinner last night, I keep coming back to it. I'm taking that as a sign the idea has merit. *Another sign – shit.* I don't know if it's the thin air at this altitude or my subconscious telling me I'm ready for a change, but the longer I'm here the more signs I see, and since they're all pointing in a direction I'm happy to go, I guess I'll keep paying attention to them.

Unfortunately, following my signs means for the first time in my life my path might not be the same one as Axel's. I always figured that would happen eventually, though it's coming sooner than expected. And even if I do pursue my own thing, I could envision a way to partner with Axel on some aspects of his gig. Maybe that would make our paths separate yet parallel instead of completely divergent. Either way, I'll still help Axel get his venture off the ground. After that, well, we'll cross that bridge as we get there. For now we'll just concentrate on making his vision a reality.

"Who's the contractor you got to build the track?" I ask as the two of us look over the plans he picked up this morning.

"Lennon's friend Cade. He gave me a bro deal."

"What sort of deal?" I cast him a sideways glance. Bro deals can be epic or awful. Sometimes the favor is genuine, and comes scot-free. Others, they come with a hidden *I Owe You.* "Cade gets lifetime access to the track when it isn't in use in exchange for building it." He lowers the blueprints just enough that he can peer over the top of them, I'm assuming so he can picture what's on the paper in the space in front of him.

"And that's a good deal because?"

"He's got all sorts of equipment to build and maintain the track, so it'll save a ton of money up front."

"That doesn't sound too bad." I relax my shoulders a bit, knowing Axel didn't just make a colossal error in his excitement to get things going.

"Gotta love small towns." He grins. "No way you can make a deal like that in a big city."

"Sounds like you're really loving it here?" I lean against the wall of the barn—arena—and watch him spin around to orient himself. It's sort of amusing to watch him try to match a 2D image with a 3D space.

"What's not to love? The trails are epic, the people are cool, and Lennon's here. Speaking of people." He turns to look at me over his shoulder. "Some of them are saying that they saw a strange car parked at your place last night."

"Don't tell me you're into small town gossip now." I deflect, taking a page from his book when he first met Lennon.

"Just cause I don't spread it doesn't mean I don't hear it. Who spent the night?" He pins me with a look that says *gotcha*.

"A friend. And she didn't spend the night. She was just there to hang out."

"By hang out you mean fuck?" His wry grin is a reminder that he knows me all too well.

"Why would you assume that?" I keep up with the innocent ruse.

"Because I *assume*, your friend is the one I saw you talking to up at the resort that day we moved boxes for Lennon. You two looked pretty cozy."

"We have a history." I nod.

Axel goes back to trying to decipher the plans now that he's got his confirmation. "What does Blake think about that? She's his boss, right?"

"Blake's got a history with her, too." That gets his attention. His hands drop to his side, crinkling the plans against his legs as he looks at me with wide eyes. "No shit? That's some fucked up luck right there."

"Actually, I think it's pretty good luck." I run a hand nervously through my hair.

"How do you figure?" He snorts. "Sleeping with the same girl your boyfriend formerly slept with sounds awkward as fuck."

"Not if the three of us are together. Then it's easy." I shrug with more confidence than I feel. Axel may know all about my preferences, but up until now I've never been so forthcoming about how those preferences sometimes *intersect*.

"The three of you together... You mean, like you all date each other?" His brows draw together, but his expression is one of confusion, not disgust.

"Eventually. Right now, just Blake and I are dating, but we're hoping to date Becca if she's up for it."

His expression doesn't change, not that I expected it to. "No more hiding, then? Blake's out?"

"Not yet." I shake my head. "We don't want to overwhelm her with relationship talk, so we're just hanging out casually for now."

Axel scratches the bridge of his nose, almost as if he's stalling to search for the best way to object. "You mean you want her to be part of a trio when she doesn't know you and Blake are a duo?"

I flex my jaw defensively, ready to retort, though I have to admit hearing it out loud sounds pretty bad. How do I explain that it's not what he thinks?

"Yeah, it sounds shitty. I'll give you that. It's not meant to be, though. Blake and I both really like her, and we want her to be with us. This lifestyle won't be easy, so we're trying to work up to the dating part."

"By fucking?" He arches a brow.

"Like you didn't start off just fucking Lennon before you fell for her?" I match his look.

Axel closes his eyes and lets out a heavy breath. "Fair enough. But you yourself just said this lifestyle is hard, and your boyfriend is still in the closet. If he won't come out for you, what makes you think he'd come out for you *and* her? And what about Becca? What happens when she finds out you haven't told her the truth?"

All valid points, which I'm trying not to dwell on myself. But there's no denying the potential for one or more of us to get hurt if we aren't on the same page. I only hope we're working toward that by first exploring the physical, which like I said, worked pretty well for Axel.

"I know it's not ideal, but I'm balancing things the best way I know how." I pop my jaw.

"These secrets are gonna burn you, Jace. Don't fool yourself into thinking they won't." He shakes his head, a solemn warning. "Are they worth it?"

"Yeah." I let my head fall back against the wall. "Yeah, I think they are."

Chapter 19

Becca

Carter's office is beautiful. So much so, that I'm a little worried he'll have to call in a cleaning crew after I leave, given that I've got dirt in every nook, cranny and crevice on my body. Perks of working outdoors.

I take a seat in the leather chair he gestures to, facing him over the expanse of his cherry wood desk. It's framed by a massive window overlooking Katah Vista mountain. I suppose if you're not going to work outside, this view is the next best thing.

Wiping my sweaty palms on my shorts, I wait for him to finish his call. Carter didn't make me nervous the first time we met, but something about the antique desk between me and his commanding tone has my stomach in knots. Or maybe it's not the man himself for the fact I slept with his employee—*my* employee, twice now—that has me off kilter.

Not only that, but I fucked both him *and* his roommate at the same time.

Just like the first time with each of them, they made me feel special. Cherished. How that's possible in the midst of something that seems like it should be taboo I have no idea, but there's no doubt in my mind it's true. Blake was gentle and observant, reading and responding to my silent cues. Jace was patient, yet commanding, providing the guidance and instruction that ensured all of us were satisfied. Together they made the experience beautiful in spite of the forbidden nature of things, and it worked out so well I can honestly say my body wants more. My heart, on the other hand, is hesitant.

I already caught a case of the feels for each of them the first time we were together, though I was rational enough not to dwell on it. I accepted that those were special moments not special beginnings, mainly because they couldn't be the beginning of anything at the time.

Last night falls into the former category. It was one night. One incredible, mind-blowing, perfect night, but ultimately just one. If I keep it up, I could see it becoming the latter in my mind, which is a problem considering there's *two* of them. I can't have a special beginning with two people. Right?

Of course, I can't. That's ridiculous. Does that mean I should stop this thing now before I develop feelings for both of them? Probably. Definitely. Will I? That's...

"Sorry about that." I jump when the receiver hits its cradle with a crack. "The forest service wants to push back our opening date because of some bird migration. What birds in the air have to do with snow on the ground is beyond me, but they're afraid the overlap would hurt the birds. "If it's not one thing..." Carter trails off, shaking his head with frustration.

"I'm sorry. Should I come back another time?" There's nothing worse than meeting with someone who's in a bad mood before you even start to speak.

"No, let's hear the update on the bike park. I need some good news."

That I can do. A relieved smile spreads across my face. "I've got lots of that. The first trail, which we've nicknamed Grasshopper, is about twenty-five percent done. It starts off with some nice switchbacks that weave down the steeper terrain at the top, a safer option than pointing the trail straight downhill, and it will finish with some long, rolling straightaways toward the bottom. We're on track to finish that by the end of the season as sort of a preview to what we're bringing to the mountain."

"Good, good." He nods, pausing so I can continue.

"We're also making progress on the path for the trails we'll be starting on next season. The switchbacks turned out so well on Grasshopper that we'd like to duplicate them on a blue or even a black run, only with taller berms to accommodate higher speeds. The goal will be to create a luge effect so bikers can ride the wall of the trail. Closer to the base area, the trail will end in a series of jumps, rollers for the blue trails and table-tops for black."

"You'll have clear signage to indicate which trails are which? I don't want a green rider ending up on a black trail." Carter's tone is firm, leaving no doubt safety is his top priority. I respect that.

"Yes, sir. Plus, the trails won't merge, so unless a rider cuts between trails there shouldn't be any crossover where people end up on a route that's too advanced for them."

"Sounds like everything is on schedule. And what about you? How are you doing?" Though his eyes are gentle his stare is intense, setting me on edge.

He doesn't... He couldn't... There's no way he could know, right?,

"I'm..." I swallow under the weight of his gaze. "I'm doing well."

"Have you met anyone yet or explored the town?" Though he can't be too much older than me, he's making me feel like a parent asking their kid if they've finished their homework.

"I went to Murphy's?" It comes out like a question, causing blood to rush to my cheeks.

"Best fries in town." Carter grins. I return it with a shy smile of my own.

"So, listen." He leans forward, resting his forearms on the desk. "It wasn't that long ago I moved here and spent the first year holed up here in the resort, thinking I had too much work on my plate to do anything else. I don't want you to make my same mistake. Make sure to get out and experience the town. There's nowhere else like it."

My heartbeat returns to normal with the realization that Carter's only looking out for me, not speculating about my private life, and I give him a genuine smile. "I will. Promise."

Scooting off the chair, I give him a tiny wave then head several floors down to my office, where Blake's waiting patiently in the chair next to my desk. *Shit – I totally forgot I told him to be here before the whole sex with two gorgeous men thing came up.*

I've never really had to do the morning after – extended scenes version – before. Usually it's the CliffsNotes version, where you wake up together and have a hug or kiss goodbye. What's the protocol for waking up alone and going to work with the guy who watched me fuck someone else while I sucked him off? Is there any way to do this without turning the color of a tomato, because red and pink don't mix so well.

"Hey." I stride past him and take a seat at my desk, casting him what I hope is a normal-ish smile. At least I think it is since he doesn't point it out.

"How'd things go with Carter this morning? Is he happy with the progress so far?"

"Fine. Yeah." My leg bounces uncontrollably under the desk though I plow forward since trying to stop it would only draw more attention. "I explained how we marked the trails, went through the timeline. We talked about... What are you doing?" My eyes track Blake as he jumps up and strides toward the door.

"Giving us some privacy." It clicks shut.

"What for?" My knee bounces faster, despite the fact I'm no longer fueling it with oxygen.

"So, you'll relax." He rounds the desk and kneels before me, resting a hand on my leg to keep it still as his hazel eyes search mine. "Please don't freak out around me."

"I can't help it. I keep thinking about last night."

"Do you regret it?" Now he's the one holding his breath.

Images flash through my mind on a loop; warm hands, soft lips, breathless cries. And the sensation of being protected. Safe. How could I regret that?

"No." I shake my head even as I feel blood rushing to my cheeks.

"Are you embarrassed?"

"A little." I press my lips together and focus on the hand caressing my knee. *I'm aroused, too, though I'll keep that part to myself.*

"Why?" he asks softly.

I'm tempted to make something up to protect what's left of my virtue, but a tiny peek at Blake's expression reveals curiosity and concern, not judgment, which has me re-thinking the need to deflect.

"Why?" he asks again.

"Because I liked it." It's easier to say that to his hand than his face, but it's the truth.

Blake tips my chin up so I'm forced to meet his eyes. "I liked it, too. More than I expected I would. So did Jace, although he never had any doubts. He's...more *experienced*." He offers an awkward shrug.

No surprise there—they did suggest it—but it's nice to know all the same.

"Does that mean we keep doing this? The three of us all the time." My gaze darts awkwardly between Blake's face and the floor, the door, even the desk, as I wait for his answer. *Will I ever be comfortable talking about this?*

"It doesn't have to be all the time." His calm tone gives me the strength to meet his stare. "It can be you and I, or you and Jace if we aren't all in the same place for some reason. But when we are together it'd be the three of us. Does that still work for you?"

My practical side sees only red flags, convinced this arrangement will result in one or more of us suffering a broken heart. My inner flamingo is telling me I've only just started flapping my wings and I should get ready to fly, which is a selfish but also much more satisfying argument.

This whole venture—new job, new town—was about getting out of the comfortable bubble I've been living in, so I might as well burst the damn thing instead of just poking a tiny hole in it, right?

"Look," Blake exhales, "this isn't where I saw things going with us, and I'd be lying if I said it feels natural to have a threesome. But I feel connected to you, and I know Jace does too, so I want to keep exploring it. I mean, if you want that."

Taking a deep breath, I give Blake a decisive nod. "Yes."

"Yeah?" A relieved smile stretches across his face. "Cool." He leans forward, planting a soft kiss on my forehead. "Now let's go build some trails. The sooner we get those done the sooner I get to ride them with you, and Jace says you're pretty sexy on a bike."

My heartbeat accelerates under his praise, and my inner flamingo revels like the badass she is.

Chapter 20

Blake

After the slightly awkward morning-after several days ago, Becca and I found a comfortable rhythm at work, fine tuning the sections of trail that have been excavated by the crew. Even better, the three of us have settled into a nightly routine of dinner and *entertainment* before we call it a night. Most times the entertainment is sex, but sometimes it's a game of cards or even watching some of the videos Jace has filmed. The only thing that would make it better is if Becca slept over, though admittedly that would start talk we haven't even addressed ourselves.

Several conversations have to take place between the three of us—sooner rather than later—so we can decide what to tell people and when. That's unfortunate since things are going really well in their undefined state, but if we ever hope to make things official, which Jace and I do, we'll have to talk about what the three of us are to each other. I'm both excited and terrified for that discussion.

Jace hasn't touched me during sex since that first night, so while I don't have a reason to think Becca would object to the two of us being involved, we don't know enough to think she'd be okay with it, either. One thing's for sure, the longer we go without addressing it the worse things will be, so something has to happen, and quickly. I'm just not sure whether we should bring it up in conversation or *"get lost"* in the moment while the three of us are together as a way to open that door.

Either way, Jace and I agree it makes sense for the town to get used to seeing the three of us together, and the concert in the park tonight is the perfect excuse. No one will think twice about me bringing my new roommate and boss to the event, and the three of us can do something outside the confines of my house. Win, win. Now I just have to convince Becca.

"You want to take me on a date? Both of you, together?" She pauses mid-shovel with a leery expression when I casually mention the invite while we're clearing the trail.

"I want you to come with us to the weekly concert in the park." I very specifically didn't say *date,* but it's interesting that's what she heard. I'll have to tell Jace.

"Is that a good idea?" She dumps the loose dirt to the side and scoops up another.

"Why wouldn't it be?" I lean on my shovel, waiting for her to look at me.

"I didn't think this thing with all of us extended beyond... you know." She talks to her shovel as she works, though I can see the pink creeping into her cheeks under the brim of her ball cap. It's cute that she still gets flustered talking about our arrangement when she's anything but when the three of us are together. "And I barely know anyone here. What will they think if we show up together?"

"They won't jump to you sleeping with both of us if that's what you're asking."

Her nose crinkles as she squints up at me. "How can you be sure? I know how small towns work, and my car has been parked at your house a lot recently."

"Your car is easy to explain. We're trying to make progress on the bike park; I'm trying to be friendly since you're new in town; take your pick. Besides, it's not there overnight, and even if you were to stay over that's easy to explain, too. You crashed on the couch because you were exhausted."

"They'd buy that I stayed over platonically instead of driving ten minutes home?" She shakes her head with an exaggerated eye roll.

"We could always say you had too much to drink."

"I hate that that actually sounds better."

My shovel falls to the ground as I step toward her and take her hand in mine. "Are you having second thoughts about this?"

"No." Thank God. She sounds confident. "But I'm not ready to have my private life on display. I'd feel that way no matter what, not because of our..." She waves her hand around instead of finishing that thought. *She's cute in her little hat with a smudge of dirt on her cheek.*

Wrapping my arms around her waist I pull her to me, her shovel clattering to the ground. "I get it. It's different, and people don't always accept different well."

She has no idea how closely that hits home for me. It's on the tip of my tongue to tell her—to get everything out in the open—and while a conversation needs to happen, I think having it within the first few days is rushing it.

It might scare her off to learn that our motives were just as much about the connection we feel to her as they were about lust, especially since lust seems to be a primary motivator for her. So, for now, keeping this about sex feels safe. Besides, I feel like she needs to be able to talk about the three of us without blushing before we bring up dating. Still, I'm taking the fact she used the word *date* as a sign we're moving in the right direction.

"I'm not suggesting different is bad. You know that, right?" She worries her lip between her teeth.

"I know that. You just want to be known as Becca and not the girl sleeping with two roommates. Plus, you're not the type of person to make everyone jealous of all the amazing sex you're having, so out of respect for them we'll pretend we're nothing more than friends."

Becca slaps a hand to her mouth to stifle the bark of laughter she couldn't quite contain, and I have to bite the inside of my cheek to stop my mouth from stretching into a proud grin for making her laugh. "Come here." I wrap my hand around the back of her neck and pull her to me, wiping the smudge off her cheek with my thumb before sealing my lips over hers. It's a firm, brief kiss since we're out in the open, but it has my chest heaving with desire all the same.

"Tonight, we're three friends hanging out. No one will say more than that, and even if they do it wouldn't be malicious. There's just not much else to talk about here other than what activity the weather is good for and what people are doing on any given day." I'm not sure if I'm trying to convince her or myself with those words, but they do the trick.

She pulls out of my grasp with a shy smile and retrieves her shovel. "Okay. I'm in."

***

A mixture of relief and excitement floods my veins when I spot Becca weaving through the crowd, making her way toward us. Heads turn to follow her movements, which may be due to the pink hair, but for me it's the way she looks both sporty and delicate in her casual overalls with a tight little top that draws my attention. It's so uniquely *her* that it's hard not to stare. A quick peek at Jace tells me the same thought is running through his mind, and I elbow him in the ribs as I swallow down my own reaction, hoping no one noticed our momentary lapse.

"Hi." She stuffs her hands in her pockets and rocks back on her heels as she stops before us, eyes darting back and forth like she's unsure what to do next. Before I can panic, Jace leans in to give her a brief hug hello.

"Glad you made it." He pulls away and steps aside, both of them looking to me for guidance. At a loss for words, I motion for them both to follow me and spin toward the direction of my usual spot, where the rest of my friends should be gathering. They all look up as the three of us approach—new people have that effect—and of course Deacon, playboy that he is, jumps right up to greet Becca.

"Pink Panty Dropper, nice to see you again." He squeezes by me to give her a hug.

"We haven't established that as my drink." She shoves his chest—playfully—though it has the effect of putting some distance between them.

"We'll see." He gives her a sly wink as he saunters back to his blanket.

"You remember Deacon." I roll my eyes, shaking loose the blanket I'm holding and dropping it to the ground before I point to the tiny blonde sitting next to him. "And Tiff. Then there's Ryder, Cade and Cora, and Finn and Ally. Guys, this is Becca, and you remember Jace."

Becca offers a tiny wave while Jace fist bumps the guys, who he met during his first trip here with Axel. Then he hands us each a beer as we all sit down.

"Where's Lennon?" Becca asks Tiff as she crosses her legs on the blanket.

"She's working. We alternate who works on concert nights so neither of us miss all of them."

"And Axel?" Becca turns to Jace. "I was hoping to meet the guy you work with."

"He's probably in Lennon's office, hoping for a quickie when she takes a break... What?" Tiff looks around at the shocked faces. "Haven't you guys seen the new couch she put in there? It's not just so he can watch the TV she installed."

"Language," Cade admonishes as he lunges at Tiff to ruffle her hair.

She dodges his advance. "What did I say?" she cries.

"That's how rumors get started." Cade throws a handful of grass at her since he couldn't muss her up.

"It's not a rumor if it's true." She untangles a piece of grass from her hair. "And what's so bad about Axel wanting to hook up with his girlfriend anyway? They're hot for each other."

"Nothing wrong with that," Deacon backs her up with a wink that makes her cheeks turn pink.

"Don't encourage her." Cade shakes his head at Deacon.

"She's got a point, though," Deacon objects. "Who cares if we know what goes on behind that door."

"Cade doesn't want Tiff talking about it because he doesn't want anyone talking about her that way. It's a brother thing." Ryder sips from the flask in his hand as we all fall into a stunned silence. It's sort of rare for him to speak up nowadays, much less make such a coherent statement.

"Self-appointed brother," Tiff mumbles under her breath, although I'm not sure Cade hears it. His focus is on Ryder, whose eyes are closed as his finger taps the flask in rhythm to the music drifting over the crowd.

A throat clears on the other side of me, and I shift to see Finn extending his hand to Becca. "Hi. I'm Finn, and this is my wife, Ally." He tilts his head toward the redhead sitting next to him.

"Finn's the Director of Operations at the resort. And your counterpart on the snow side," I explain as Becca shakes his hand. "He's building some black runs on the back side of the mountain we're cutting trails on."

"Sorry, I wasn't around your first day. We took a little trip for our anniversary and just got back. I can't wait to see what you're working on."

Becca darts a glance toward Jace, who's now deep in conversation with Deacon, before offering Finn a warm smile. "Sounds like you have a pretty interesting project going on as well. And I think Lennon mentioned you the other day," she says to Ally. "Something about owning your own business?"

"I have a boutique on Main Street. You should stop by. I have a jumper that would look great on you."

"Really? That's great." Becca's tone is friendly, though I can hear the subtle hesitation in her voice. I'm assuming that stems from the fact that her style isn't anything like Ally's, who doesn't include the word casual in her vocabulary.

"Ally likes to dress everyone, especially for costume events. It's sort of her hobby," Finn smiles bashfully.

"She dresses you?" Becca gives my t-shirt and shorts a once-over as if to say, *'This is what she picked?'*

I bark out a laugh as Ally rolls her eyes. "The guys only let me dress them in costume. Or for special occasions. They all assume I'm going to make them wear something they don't like just because *I* think it looks good."

"Ah, gotcha." Becca visibly relaxes now that Ally's put that particular fear to rest.

Figuring it's safe to leave Becca with her now that she knows a full makeover is off the table, I excuse myself to visit with Ryder.

"Hey." His cloudy eyes track me as I sit, pulling my knees up so I can prop my forearms on them. "Bike park's coming along, you should come check it out."

He looks at me with a blank expression.

"Remember how Carter talked about making lift accessible bike trails on the mountain?" I try again. "We're doing that now. Me and Becca." I jerk my head in her direction, and though his head stays still, I'm pretty sure his eyes shift. "Swing by tomorrow and I'll show you."

"Not interested." He takes another sip of his drink.

A month ago, I think he would've been—the idea of a downhill run without having to pedal uphill first would be appealing to a guy who makes a living letting gravity do the hard work—but I get that maybe it's too soon after his brother's death for him to feel excited about the new park.

"Okay, if you don't want to see the park then let's hit the trail. We haven't done that in a while."

"Can't."

Ryder's always been more of a winter sports guy, so it's possible he's not feeling the bike right now. Although, his indifference has me a little worried. He's too active of a guy to sit around moping all the time, even if he is in mourning.

"Well, if you don't want to do anything for fun, maybe you could help me work. We're trying to get this new trail done before the season's over, and I could use the extra hands." It's a lame idea, but at least it would get him moving outside.

"I don't need the money."

"I'm not saying you do. I'm saying I could use your help."

"Sorry. I've got other shit to do. I gotta take a leak." He pops up with more energy than I expect, given the unfocused look in his eye, and stalks toward the public bathrooms near the playground adjacent to the park. Though his gait isn't smooth, he doesn't appear to be staggering. Still, I don't like the look of it, which must show on my face.

"Don't take it personally." Deacon's voice interrupts my thoughts. "I'm pretty sure the last time he was on a bike was with Chase. I think it's the bike he's got issues with, not you."

"Whatever it is, time doesn't seem to be making things better." I can't seem to relax my brows even though Ryder's now out of sight.

"Is there some sort of time limit on grief I'm not aware of?"

I open my mouth to respond but nothing comes out. I've never lived through loss, so I'm not exactly an expert on it, which I assume is Deacon's point.

"I hear you," I concede. "Keep an eye on him though, yeah?"

"Of course." Deacon's voice is steady, but the way his gaze roams over the crowd—like he's looking for his next conquest—doesn't give me much faith in his word.

Chapter 21

Jace

Blake's shoulders slump as his friend Ryder walks away, and it takes all of my willpower not to go over and put my arm around him. Instead, I lift my brows in a silent question, and get a slight head nod in return. It'll have to do for now.

I think back to the first time I met Blake and his friends—sitting at the bar watching a mountain bike competition during my first trip here—and they had to leave early to take Ryder home. Blake said Ryder was trying to drink himself numb after the death of his brother, which had happened only days before. Based on Blake's expression, it seems like that's still Ryder's mission. I'm not surprised Blake would try to engage him in conversation and assume blame when he couldn't pull Ryder out of his own head. I just wish I didn't have to pretend to be oblivious to Blake's pain right now.

Fortunately, Becca's cheery voice seems to grab his attention as she tells the other girls about what she's doing on the mountain, and he perks up a little bit. In that instant, my body rattles like the echo of the bass just passed through me, only that can't be right since there's hardly any bass in this song. *Holy shit—was that my heart?*

Propping my elbows on my knees, I discreetly rub my hand over my chest, feeling the steady yet rapid thump coming from inside. *Well, shit.* I take a shaky breath as clarity washes over me, settling into my veins in a warm, comfortable hum. *I'm in love. With both of them*

Seeing the way Becca lightened Blake's mood—instead of being jealous or upset that she could ease his pain when I couldn't, I felt relieved. Proud even. It was confirmation of my deepest belief—that the three of us are perfect for each other—which gives me hope that it's only a matter of time before we can be done hiding.

Blake casts a quick glance my way—he must've felt me staring. He sucks in a breath when his eyes meet mine, and I'd be shocked if he doesn't know exactly what I'm thinking right now. While this isn't how I wanted him to find out, I don't regret that he knows. I want him to.

I'm not sure how long we stare at each other. Too long, I'm sure. I can only hope everyone was too focused on the girls' conversation to notice.

"You're saying that even though I'm not a very strong rider, I'll be able to do the green trails?" Cora asks Becca.

"Absolutely." Becca bobs her head up and down. "Green trails are mostly just dirt—no obstacles and nothing technical—just a nice flowy ride."

"You could do that." Finn nudges Ally's arm with his elbow.

"I *could*," she agrees. "But I'm not sure I will. Snow is much more forgiving than dirt."

"Powder is. Hardpack though?" Becca shudders. "I'd rather fall on dirt."

Everyone looks my way when I laugh, and I'm forced to admit I agree, which starts a debate about how we'd prefer to crash, biking or boarding. I'm not sure it makes Ally any more likely to get on a bike, but by the end of the evening both Cora and Tiff have agreed to ride with Becca, and that has our girl beaming. The only thing that would make the night better is if I could tell everyone she, and Blake, are mine. *Soon – I hope, especially now that there's no turning back for me.*

It's not my place to say, but I get the sense Blake's friends wouldn't give our little threesome a second thought. They all seem pretty chill, and aside from Tiff commenting about what Lennon and Axel get up to in the office, the night wasn't filled with gossip. Besides, Tiff's words didn't strike me as malicious. I almost think they held envy, like she wants what Lennon has. Not Axel. Just... *someone*.

Come to think of it, her comments remind me a little of Blake. The way he was sort of resigned to choosing one way of life because it was convenient instead of chasing what he really wanted. It makes me wonder what it is that she wants and thinks she can't have, and whether Blake, Becca, and I can show her anything's possible.

After the concert, a few people wander toward Main Street to grab drinks at the bar, but when Blake and I decline, Becca offers to drive us home. It's the perfect excuse to leave together, though I have no plans to let her drop us and go. Not after watching them both all evening without being able to touch them.

We barely make it through the front door before Becca spins and rises on her toes to give me a kiss, swiping her tongue along mine only once before she turns to Blake and presses her lips to his. *Tease.*

"Bedroom. Now," I growl, smacking her playfully on the ass as she takes off down the hallway with the two of us trailing behind her. The second she disappears through the door, I take advantage of the few seconds Blake and I have alone, pressing him against the wall and crushing our mouths together. I brush my thumb over his jaw as our tongues collide in a frenzy of need, pouring everything I can't yet say into the press of my lips against his. I break the connection before either of us can even moan, giving him a soft, swift kiss as I pull away. It's not what he deserves after my silent confession earlier, but now isn't the time to say the words to either of them.

Becca waits for us at the foot of the bed, and as I reach her, I devour her mouth while slipping the overalls off her shoulders. Then I spin her to face Blake and lift her tank top over her head before unhooking her bra, exposing her soft skin to him.

Cupping her breasts from behind, I mold them in my hand as Blake stalks forward, his eyes darting from mine to what my hands are doing. I can sense he's struggling, conflicted about taking Becca to bed amid the truth I realized tonight. One I suspect—hope—he shares. Then she moans as I pinch her nipples, and heat flares across his face.

"Our girl's beautiful, isn't she?" I ask him as I nuzzle the side of her neck.

"Hell yes." His head dips to take her mouth, smothering the gasp she makes.

Trapped between us, nearly naked, Becca leans her head back against my chest as Blake and I trail our fingers over her body. Her collarbone, her stomach, her thighs—everywhere we can reach we caress, loving the feel of her soft body next to ours.

Becca's ass rocks against me as she steps out of the panties Blake drags down her hips, shooting a jolt of electricity through my already engorged cock. I spin her so she's facing me and palm her ass, rubbing the backs of my hands against Blake's dick as I squeeze her round little cheeks. He returns the favor, brushing his knuckles over my shaft as he circles her clit. It feels incredible, her delicate body sandwiched between us, the three of us writhing together. But guilt over straining for Blake's fingers without Becca's knowledge overtakes me, and I step away with a strangled moan.

"Get naked and get on the bed, Blake. I want to watch you two fuck." Becca's thighs clench as she licks her lips, which has me shedding my own clothes and taking my dick in hand.

Stroking leisurely—just to take the edge off—I watch as Blake licks his fingers then strips off his shorts and climbs on the bed.

"Lean against the headboard," I tell him.

Becca moves to follow, but I clasp my hands around her waist to hold her still until he's situated. "Look how hard he is already." I kiss up the side of her neck as he watches us, dick pointing to the sky. "Think you can make him even harder?" I reach around her to strum my fingers over her clit, teasing.

"How?" Her chest rises with a deep inhale.

"Lick him from balls to tip, then take him in your mouth." I whisper against her ear, just loud enough for Blake to hear. His cock bobs as his stomach tenses in anticipation, muscles rippling as they contract.

Becca crawls forward on all fours, sticking that cute little ass in the air as she lowers her head. I watch, transfixed, as Blake's eyes flutter closed when the heat of her mouth surrounds him. The tendons in his neck flex as he locks his jaw, his chest stills. His fingers claw at the sheets while her head bobs slowly up and down, caressing his perfect cock with her tongue.

His expression is a mixture of bliss and restraint, soaking up the pleasure even as he fights to keep it at bay. Its fucking mesmerizing and hot as shit.

Leaning forward, I run my hand up the inside of Becca's thigh, dipping a finger into her core. Silky heat surrounds me, and I pump my finger back and forth, coating myself in her essence before slicking it over her clit. As I stroke that sensitive little bud, she moans around Blake's cock, and his hips buck underneath her. Lifting a hand from the sheets, he threads his fingers in her hair and cradles her head in his palm, cursing softly as she loves on his cock.

Their bodies move together in sync, savoring the connection between them. It's tender and carnal at the same time, making my chest ache with affection as my cock swells.

The three of us have come together nearly a half dozen times since that first night, and each time has been physically incredible. But none of those encounters compare to what's happening right now, watching two people I love pleasure one another.

"You're making him come undone." I slip my finger inside Becca again, loving the way her slick walls clench around me. "It's so hot, but we don't want him to finish yet. Sit up."

Her cheeks hollow as she pulls back, letting him go with an audible 'pop.'

"Good girl. Now spin around and straddle him." She sits up and moves over Blake's torso, giving him her back while positioning herself to sink onto his cock. "Condom first." She pauses as I pull a foil packet from the nightstand and hand it to her.

Resting her weight on Blake's hips with his shaft between her thighs, she fumbles with the wrapper as she rocks back and forth, straining for the friction that will ease the ache. It's so fucking hot to see her this needy, and cute too, since her desire is making her clumsy.

Blake curses as he lifts his hips, his cock full and hard and dripping with need. Becca grunts as she drops the condom, and he groans in reply. Taking matters into my own hands I grab the wrapper, tear it open, and fist Blake's dick in one hand while I position the condom with the other. He hisses as I roll it over his length and hold him ready.

"Need your pussy, Becca," he grits.

I give him a little squeeze and withdraw my hand as Becca sinks onto him, the two of them moaning as they join together.

The scent of their arousal floods my nostrils, a heady musk that makes my mouth water. Leaning down I spread Becca apart with my thumbs and place my tongue on her clit, flicking it gently back and forth as she grinds on Blake's cock.

"Holy fuck," she cries, tossing her head back as her fingers clutch my hair.

Tiny whimpers seep from her throat as I suck on her swollen nub. Blake pumps into her with shallow thrusts that will keep her on the edge without sending her over. I want so badly to let my tongue drift lower, to lick up Blake's shaft then swirl it around Becca's clit, but I hold back knowing it's not fair to do that to either of them without warning. Instead, I savor Becca's pussy, lapping up her essence, until Blake signals she's on the brink.

"Damn, she just got tight. You want her to come on your cock or mine?" Blake's hands grip her hips as he grinds slowly into her.

"Yours." I kneel so my face is level with Becca's. "I want to come in your mouth, beautiful. Can I?" I stroke her cheek.

She nods, and I give her a tender kiss before she leans forward, lining her mouth up to my dick. I inch forward, trying not to move too fast despite the desperate need to pump my hips like an animal. When I hit the back of her throat, I lift my eyes to Blake's. His tongue swipes across his bottom lip. Then we start to move.

Gentle at first, we take turns thrusting so that only one of us is inside her at a time, Blake rubbing her clit while I play with her tits. Wet heat surrounds me as she moans on my shaft, sending sparks of electricity from my balls to my toes. It feels incredible, the slide of her tongue over my skin, the pull of her lips as she sucks. But it's Blake's gaze that has me reeling.

The emotion in his eyes, desire, awe, *love*... It's my undoing. Cupping Becca's head in my hands, I caress her cheeks as I burst, and my cum shoots down her throat. Blake holds her to him, fingers pressing her swollen bud as he grunts through his release while a muffled shout accompanies hers, the vibrations dragging out my own orgasm.

Dazed yet buzzing, I somehow register that I need to pull away so Becca can breathe. Breaking the connection leaves a physical ache in my chest even as the last jolts of aftershocks ripple through me, and it takes my remaining strength to flop down next to Blake on the bed instead of collapsing on top of them both.

Becca's arms give out and she drops to the mattress, still impaled on Blake's dick. He loosens his grip on her hips, trailing his hands over her thighs as his chest rises and falls with ragged breaths.

Seconds stretch into minutes, the three of us too content—too spent—to move. Or speak. It's not awkward, but it's not comfortable, either. We all know this moment is temporary—soon Becca will get up to leave regardless of the fact that I'm fairly sure none of us wants that—and when she does, I'll have to face Blake.

As if she can hear my thoughts, Becca starts to shift, freeing Blake's cock as she climbs off the bed and starts reaching for her clothes. Blake tugs the condom off and heads to the bathroom, so I reluctantly get up and grab our boxers off the floor, tossing his to him as he comes back in the room.

We pull them on as Becca finishes dressing, and the moment her clothes are back in place I pull her to me, wrapping my arms around her so her head is pressed against my chest. "I hate that you're leaving." I kiss the top of her head.

The second I drop my arms Blake takes her into his. "I hate it, too."

"You know why I am." She takes his hand in hers and gives it a subtle squeeze. "Besides, we've all got work tomorrow."

"What if we didn't?" I ask. "Would you stay?"

She worries her bottom lip with her teeth. "Maybe."

"This weekend?" I raise my eyebrows.

"We'll see." She drops Blake's hand with a coy smile and leaves the room, the two of us trailing behind her to the front door. She gives us each a sweet, lingering kiss, then makes her way outside.

As the door clicks shut, I lift my eyes to Blake's, bracing for what I might find. I'm expecting frustration or regret since I didn't stop things from getting physical when I probably should've avoided that until coming clean about my feelings. Instead, all I see is acceptance.

"You aren't upset with me?" It's barely more than a whisper.

"How could I be upset with you for feeling what I do?"

"You..."

He grabs the back of my head and brings our lips together in a bruising kiss. "Of course, I do." He rests his forehead against mine. "You know I always assumed finding *the one* would dictate what I say about my lifestyle—did you honestly think I'd be living with you if I didn't know you're it for me?"

"I mean... I hoped... Why didn't you say anything?" Pulling back, I search his face for the clues I'm obviously missing as his hand drops to his side.

"I didn't want to scare you."

"Why would I be scared?"

"Because I fell for you the first night," he says softly. "Seeing you again in Utah after I'd been thinking about you since the first time I saw you... It felt sort of meant to be. And that's not the sort of thing you admit right away. Then you showed up here and I knew."

"Why the secrecy then? I'm not mad," I rush to clarify, "just confused."

He puts his hand over my heart, rubbing gentle circles over my pec with his thumb. "Part of it was not knowing what to say to people or how to say it. Part of it was wanting to make sure you felt the same way first."

"I do." I clasp his hand in mine, holding it against my chest. "I think it was there all along and I was afraid to trust it since it happened so fast, but I'm not worried about that anymore. I love you."

"And Becca? Do you love her too?"

"I'm pretty sure you know I do."

"Me, too." He drops his head to my shoulder. "Are we fucked? Being in love with someone who doesn't know we love each other?"

"I refuse to believe that." I lift his head off me and cup his face in my hands so he can see the truth in my eyes. "Her being here, with us, is meant to be, just like you and I are."

A look of panic ghosts across his face. "Do you think she'll believe that? I mean, I'm not sure this is just sex for her, but that doesn't mean she's all in with *this*." He draws a line between the two of us. "I know we need to tell her how we feel, but do we start with that, or with the two of us being together? I don't want to scare her away."

"One day at a time, remember?" I kiss his forehead. "And if it makes you feel better, we can tell her about us before we tell her we love her."

"You mean tell her we're together?" He lets out a shaky breath.

"Or tell her we're bi. Seeing the two of us together might open the door for her to consider that this can be more than sex, for all of us."

"Okay." He sucks in a lungful of air. "Dammit, I'm scared. I want this to work so bad."

"It will." I lean in to give him a reassuring kiss. "I love you, Blake."

"I love you, too." Those four little words give me hope that the life I dreamed of is about to become reality.

Chapter 22

Becca

Liz's name flashes on the display, bringing a smile to my face as I hit *accept*. "Hey sis. How are my little nephews doing?"

Charlie and Henry are two and four, and after they had to move to Arizona for my brother-in-law's job I haven't seen much of them. Had they stayed in Utah I might not have taken a job in Katah Vista, even if it made me one of the first female bike park designers on record. Them being gone was just one more reason for me to try something new, too.

"They're doing great. They miss their auntie."

"I miss them. So, are you boiling in the desert sun?" My sister is neither a tomboy nor an outdoor lover, but with two little boys she can't escape playtime outside. I never get tired of teasing her about that.

"I actually took them to an indoor pool the other day, thank you very much."

"It's August for you too, right? You didn't go through some sort of time portal or something when you crossed the border, because if I remember correctly, August is summer. No indoor pools allowed.

"When it's seventy-five degrees indoors and well over a hundred outdoors, you'd stay inside, too. Besides, you'll probably get snow in the next few weeks, and when you do, you'll be begging to come down here and borrow my sunshine."

I roll my eyes even though she's right. "I just might take you up on that. So, have you met any more people down there?"

"I signed Henry up for preschool, so I'm sure I'll meet some other moms soon. What about you?"

A smile tugs at my mouth as I recall the concert a few nights back. Not only did I meet some really friendly girls, they've already invited me to brunch this weekend. "Actually, yes. There's a group of girls here that seem pretty nice, *and* they like biking. Or they're willing to try, anyway. One of them, Tiff, grew up here so she's done some riding before. Then there's Cora, her husband has been teaching her to bike, but she'd like a girlfriend to ride with. The others seem interested in having me teach them, too."

"Sounds like you found your people." I hear the joy in Liz's voice, and I have to swallow down the lump it makes in my throat.

Only Liz knows the extent of my loneliness in Utah, and how I struggled to find people there. I clung to Brian pretty hard after our parents died in a car wreck, and my friendships suffered because of it. It didn't help that I buried myself in work, establishing myself as the person Jackson could rely on. It was amazing for my career but the kiss of death for my social life. By the time I picked my head up from the bike trail and realized Brian was cheating on me, most of my friends had moved away or moved on. So, I did what was familiar. More work.

Looking back, I can't say I regret anything. Those choices paved the way for this job, and I'm grateful to have it. But I've also learned that no matter how much I love my job I have to balance living with working, and finding people I can relate to is a great start.

"It's early still, but yeah. I can see myself being happy here."

"So, you've met some girls. What about guys?" The silence tells me she's holding her breath, waiting for my response.

I should've been expecting this question. Liz has been wanting me to get back out there for months, not because she thinks I need a man but because she doesn't want me to be afraid of them. I sort of figured she'd give me more time to get settled before bringing guys up, though.

Guys. It's on the tip of my tongue to tell her yes, I've met some. But I can't get the words out.

"You have met someone." I hear the sly smile in her voice.

"I didn't say that."

"Your silence says it all."

"Hardly," I mutter under my breath as my mind wanders to *two* sexy faces.

"What was that?" *I swear the woman has bionic ears.* "You know I'll drive to Katah Vista so you can tell me in person if you don't tell me now. Who is he?"

I puff out my cheeks and exhale slowly, stalling to brace for her reaction. "Remember how I hooked up with a guy right before I got this job offer?"

"Omigosh. The sandy-haired one that was super-hot without any ego?"

"That's the one. Blake." At least she recalled the lack of ego detail. It'll make him sound better when she hears the full story.

"You hooked up with him again?" Her voice rises several octaves as her excitement mounts.

"Turns out he lives here. And works at the mountain. He was in Utah to meet with Jackson, and I missed that meeting since I was on my way back from visiting you. I just happened to run into him that night and, well, the rest you know."

"Holy wow! So you reconnected? That's amazing. I remember you telling me what a good guy he is, sort of like that one you met right after you broke up with Brian. What was his name? Jason? Josh? Something with a J."

"Jace. Yeah. So, funny story. Jace lives here, too." My palms are suddenly sweaty, and I trap the phone between my ear and my shoulder so I can wipe them on my shorts.

"Get out! I thought he traveled for his job or something."

"He does. Or did. Now, he lives here. With Blake. They're roommates." I swear my heart is about to beat out of my chest. I've never felt so anxious in my life. Not even the first time I slept with *both* the guys. That was a breeze compared to this.

"Oh crap." She sucks in a breath. "What are the odds the only two men you've had an interest in since Brian are roommates? Do they know you hooked up with both of them?"

"Yeah... They know."

"Is that awkward?" Her voice is tinged with concern.

"Not as awkward as you'd think."

"So, wait. Which one did you reconnect with?"

I wring my hands together, gathering courage. "Both," I squeak.

The line goes dead silent.

"Oh honey, oh no. You can't do that. They live together, it's going to come out that you've been with them both. Again. You don't want to be stuck in the middle of two friends."

"I'm not going behind anyone's back."

More silence. I don't know whether to be frustrated or relieved that I can't see her face to know what she's thinking.

"They know about each other?"

"Intimately." A pan clatters in the background, and I have to cover my mouth with my hand to stop the laugh from escaping. *Poor Liz.*

She probably thought I couldn't shock her any worse than I did with the pink hair.

"I'm sorry, what?"

"We sort of have an arrangement."

"*We?* As in the three of you?"

"Yep." I press my lips together and wait for her reaction.

"Are you saying what I think you're saying?"

"What do you think I'm saying?" It's not really fair, but I want her to say it instead of me.

"Don't play dumb. You're the *meat* in between their *bread?*"

Well, I prefer to think of myself as the pin cushion that they're poking holes into with their... *Okay,* maybe her analogy is better.

"Ugh. Just say threesome. That's way less creepy."

"Three...," she trails off, and I get a sudden image of her blinking in rapid succession as she turns the word over in her head. "Hold up, you said arrangement. Does that mean this is a regular thing?"

"Pretty regular."

"Oh my gosh, you have to stop right now."

"Why?" It comes out harsher than intended, but having her tell me no raises my hackles. "There's nothing wrong with three people having consensual sex."

"There is when you can't separate sex from feelings," she retorts. "It already happened with these guys once, didn't it? You thought about them long after they were gone, and that was after *one* night. What happens after three nights? Or three months? You'll be half in love with them if you aren't already."

Dammit, why do I tell her everything?

"They made a lasting impression, I'll give you that. But just because it was memorable doesn't mean I pined away for either of them after one night."

"It's not one night anymore. And it's not one guy anymore. You're going to fall for one of them and someone will get hurt."

She makes a good point—one I've already thought of since both Blake and Jace are guys I *could* see myself falling for. And yeah, maybe there's a tiny emotional component involved in the sense that the guys are so considerate when we're all together, making me feel genuinely cared for. Cherished almost. Plus, they're just as concerned for my well-being and reputation as I am, going to great lengths to portray me as a friend and nothing more. And despite our unconventional arrangement there isn't any jealousy or awkwardness between us when Blake and I tell Jace about or day, or when Jace rubbed my leg driving home while Blake sat in the back seat after the concert. All in all, they're both great guys, and hanging out with them feels natural. But none of that inherently means I've got... Oh shit.

"Tell me you haven't fallen for both of them," Liz says softly.

"Don't be ridiculous," I protest despite a nagging fear I've done just that. Jace's dark intensity and Blake's easygoing charm may speak to me in different ways, but I crave both, and I don't want to give up either. "We're all just having fun. Three single people making the most of not being tied down."

"I'm serious, Becca. I worry about you. The way you were after Brian... He broke your heart. I don't want to see you go through that again."

"Brian's *secrets* broke my heart. Blake and Jace and I don't have any secrets."

I sign off by telling Liz I've got everything under control, but I can't help wondering—is that still true if I want to be with them in *and* out of the bedroom?

Chapter 23

Blake

"That was incredible." Becca's chest heaves as she tries to catch her breath, eyes roaming over the picturesque scene in front of her. "I'm not sure which I liked more, the trail or the view."

We've just finished one of my favorite trails, which starts at a somewhat isolated summit and ends near the base of the resort. From the top there's a three-hundred-sixty-degree view of the surrounding peaks and valleys, with rolling green hills in every direction. It's impossible to describe the vastness of the landscape up there, but impressive as it is, it's only part of the beauty of this trail. The real draw—this time of year, anyway—are the wildflowers.

Pinks and purples, reds and yellows, tiny splashes of color dot the landscape in every direction, but as you get closer, winding through the fields, those flowers get big. Head high in some places. I've never seen anything else like it, and while I haven't traveled as much as Jace, I'm not unfamiliar with some great rides. Still, it's got nothing on the pink-haired beauty next to me, her eyes wide with wonder and a triumphant smile on her face. *Damn, she's incredible.*

"Definitely the view." A sly grin spreads across my face as I give her a once over.

Becca rolls her eyes playfully. "I was talking about the wildflowers."

I lean forward, putting my lips next to her ear. "I know, but your ass in those bike shorts is better than wildflowers any day." Tilting my head way to the side so our helmets don't bump, I drop a quick kiss on her plump lips. *Who knew a kiss at the end of a ride could rival the ride itself?*

"Pervert." She pushes my chest away playfully.

"I can't help it. A woman who's beautiful *and* holds her own on a bike... You kinda tick all the boxes on my fantasy checklist."

"Only two boxes on that list?" She cocks her head to the side, a challenging smirk on her face.

"I'm a simple guy."

Her hand shoots toward me, brushing the back of her knuckles over my semi-hard dick. "And a horny one."

"You have no idea," I growl, pulling her hand away from my junk before things get *really* uncomfortable and giving her fingers a squeeze. "But my cock isn't coming out while we're on the clock." *Never* thought I'd be the responsible voice about screwing around at work.

"We're on a lunch break," she objects.

"Which is almost over." I point at my watch.

"It *is* Friday." She chews on her lip as the gears in her head spin. "I bet the crew would be excited to start their weekend a few hours early. Let's call it a day."

I arch a brow in her direction. "I never pegged you for the type to be a bad influence, boss."

"I'm a great influence." Her tongue swipes her bottom lip suggestively, and I stifle back a groan.

"Yeah, great," I snort. "Tell you what, I'll give the guys the afternoon off while you put your bike away. Meet me at the house in say, an hour?"

"Deal." She squeals as I pinch her ass, then takes off toward her place. I take a minute to text Jace and fill him in on our plans so he can meet us, then ride toward the worksite, using the quiet to collect my thoughts.

Even though I could have Becca to myself for the afternoon—something I think she'd be game for and which I do eventually want—neither Jace or I has had her to ourselves since the three of us started sleeping together, and it feels strange to think about. Not wrong, but not exactly right either, given that we haven't told her we've fallen for her. Or that Jace and I have those same feelings for each other.

Becca deserves to know how we feel before things go any further. For now, that just means telling her Jace and I are bi, and that we want the three of us to date each other. It's too soon to spring the 'L' word on her. Still, I want her to know this thing between us is more than just a casual hookup. It doesn't feel right to have sex until we do that, and even though I know it's the right thing, I'm fucking terrified.

What if she doesn't like the idea of two men together physically? If she can't wrap her head around that then there's no way she'd accept the two of us dating or being in love. Or the three of us being together.

So many things can go wrong, and that doesn't include what could happen outside our little bubble.

I'm not afraid of people learning that I like men *and* women, or that I have a relationship with both—if Becca's willing to pursue that. Nervous maybe, but not because of what my secret *is* so much as the fact that I've been keeping it. My friends and family are liberal enough not to disown me or anything, but they might be offended over the fact I didn't speak up sooner. And they might be wary of me dating a man *and* a woman. Hell, I was leery of that at first, but now that I'm in it, I can't imagine life any other way.

I sort of wish I'd come to terms with my sexuality earlier. Maybe then I wouldn't have been so confused about who I was, or hidden part of myself on the off chance I'd never have to reveal it. Then I wouldn't be freaking out about what I should say.

Speaking of the big reveal, I have no idea how to approach that, with Becca or anyone else. Jace said the key is being open and honest, but that's not what I get hung up on. My roadblock comes with how to start the conversation.

Do we blurt it out, 'hey, Jace and I are bi and we like to fuck each other?' Or do I ask her to sit down and potentially freak her out and make her think I'm about to drop a bombshell on her. So far, those are the only two options I've come up with. It's either rip the band aid off or peel it back slowly. Neither sound like great choices.

And once we clear that hurdle, how do we tell her we want more? Do we throw it out casually, like '*hey, as long as we're all sleeping together why don't we date?*' Or do we skip the dating thing and go straight to '*will you be our girlfriend?*'

There's no good opening that I can see, but I have to find one, because she deserves to know where my head is at. Where *our* heads are at. And until we do that, I'm not sure it's fair to share her body.

It's hard to believe that just a few weeks ago I wasn't sold on the idea that a relationship with three people could work, and now I want it so desperately I'm nearly sick with anxiety. Jace's stable presence and Becca's limitless joy, his hard angles and her soft curves. They're the perfect compliment to each other, to me, and I need them both like I need air to breathe.

After sending the guys home, I head to the employee lockers for a quick shower, hoping it will wipe away the sweat from the trail and calm my nerves, which shifted from slightly turned on to all out panic the deeper I sunk into my thoughts. Then I hop on the bus, grateful I'm not the one driving since my leg won't stop bouncing. *Please don't let this be the end.*

Becca's and Jace's cars are already here when I get home—my shower ran long since I needed the extra time to compose myself—and I relax a bit knowing Jace's rational air and calming demeanor will help me get through the conversation I'm both impatient for and dreading. I take a deep breath and open the front door.

Beyond the tiny entry I can just make out the back of Jace's head on the couch, and hear the heavy, rhythmic breaths echoing through the room. Striding quietly forward the view opens up, and I see Becca sitting on Jace's lap, tits bouncing subtly as she grinds on his cock.

Damn. Although, I was expecting awkward conversation to come before sexy times—if sex was on the table at all—I can't complain about coming home to this. The sight of them together, completely enthralled, is mesmerizing. It makes me happy. I lean against the wall to watch.

A faint musky smell drifts through the air as their bodies come together, over and over again, colliding with a smack that echoes through the room. Becca's hands are braced on his shoulders for balance, while his roam reverently over her flushed skin, admiring every curve. She holds his gaze as if she wants to take his soul and his body into her own. It's the same way she looks at me, and it makes my cock impossibly hard inside my shorts.

Despite being an outsider in this moment, it makes me happy to see the two of them so intimately. I've seen this before of course, and just like all the other times, their arousal makes me hard. Yet the way they move together, giving and taking in sync, gives me hope that she's just as ready as we are for this to become something more, the same way we are.

That's still hard for me to believe despite feeling in my gut it's true. For years, I figured my tastes would make a relationship like this impossible. Yet, here I am, watching my boyfriend and lover of merely a few weeks, and knowing that they've already become part of me. An integral part.

The way they look at each other, the way they move together, it's hot as fuck, yeah, but it's not just my dick that reacts. It's my soul. I know how cheesy that sounds, but that doesn't make it any less true. My entire being is so full of gratitude and affection watching them together, my chest literally aches with the emotions inside it. *I love them so much.*

Becca snaps her eyes to mine when she feels my stare, a sultry little gasp frozen on her lips. Jace twists his head to follow her movement, his eyes flaring with heat when he sees me.

"You're late. Get over here and get your cock out since you're the one who got her all revved up," he commands.

I'm crossing the room and stripping my shirt off before I can stop myself. "Me? What did I do?"

Jace pauses their movements by holding Becca's hips snug against his. "What'd you say to me when you got here, beautiful?"

Her cheeks, already a slight pink from exertion, grow even pinker. "Blake said his cock doesn't come out while he's on the clock, and I'm tired of waiting."

"Then she pushed me down on the couch and pulled my dick out. Didn't you?" He presses his thumb to her clit, rubbing it in slow circles.

"Yes," she moans, pressing forward against his finger.

"Now you're caught up." Jace smirks at me. "So, get your cock out and put it in her mouth, just like she wants."

So much for no sex before conversation.

Becca lifts her baby blues to mine as her sultry little mouth opens up, and my pants drop to the floor as I place the tip of my cock on her lips. Her eyes drift closed as her tongue darts out to swirl around the head, then takes me deeper with a contented purr. *Fuck*!

After watching them together, I'm not that far behind, and the feel of Becca's warm, wet mouth sliding over my length has me instantly on edge. Running my fingers through the thick pink strands of her hair, I rock forward gently, careful not to cut off the air she needs to keep riding Jace.

"So beautiful," he murmurs as she resumes rolling her hips. "You look so beautiful between us, taking our cocks. We're so fucking lucky we found you."

I sneak a peek at Jace and find him watching, enthralled, as Becca's lips slide over me. The bliss on his face, on hers, nearly undoes me. *I never want this moment to end.*

Taking her hand from his shoulder, Jace guides it between my legs. "Play with his balls, Becca. Roll them around like this." He guides her fingers with his own, returning his hand to her clit when she has the motion down.

Jace's chest heaves as he watches Becca swallow me, hungry eyes darting between her face and mine. My gaze is drawn to his lean abs, which contract with each plunge deep inside Becca's pussy. She moans around my cock and my head falls back as I soak up the feel of her tongue, slicking over my length.

Swallowing back the urge to let go, I lift my head to look at Becca, nearly losing it again when I see her eyelids flutter as she takes me deep, like sucking my cock gives her as much pleasure as it does me. *That's fucking*... What the hell?

I pull out of her mouth with an audible pop. "What is that?"

"What?" She blinks out of her lust-filled haze.

"What?" Jace echoes as he rocks his hips upward.

"That." I try to point at the object, but Becca's back blocks the view for Jace. Apparently, he doesn't need to see my hand to know what I'm gesturing about.

"That's the other reason she's so worked up." He looks at me with hooded eyes. "Tell him." He waggles his brows at Becca.

"I uh..." she stutters. "I wanted to get ready. For both of you."

Whether from exertion or embarrassment her cheeks are bright pink, but she's never looked more beautiful to me. Or got me so excited. Up until this moment I didn't realize words could knock the wind out of you just as effectively as a wipeout.

"Holy...My bedroom. *Now*," I choke.

Jace gives Becca a firm slap on the ass and lifts her off his cock, then the three of us practically sprint to the bed.

Chapter 24

Becca

A cool shiver races up my spine despite the fact that I'm sandwiched between two warm bodies. Two hard, naked bodies, each with a rigid cock pressing against my flesh.

Hands roam over my shoulders, up my thighs, along my waist, between my legs. Reverent touches that both soothe and arouse me, making my body war with itself over contentment and impatience.

Calloused fingers caress my bare skin as soft lips nuzzle my neck, my ear, my mouth. Eyes closed, I rest my head against the body behind me—Jace—as my hands explore the one in front—Blake.

"Beautiful," a voice rasps in my ear.

"So beautiful," another echoes.

A hand clasps my chin, dragging it toward my shoulder. Warm lips cover mine, coaxing my mouth open. A tongue licks gently inside, teasing, *tasting*. Then another set of lips claims me as a low groan rumbles from behind, deep in Jace's throat.

As if on cue, both men step closer, pressing flush against me. One firm cock rests against my lower back, another my stomach. Hips grind, trapping the rigid flesh between us. I want to take them in my hands, stroking my thumb over their velvety tips as I squeeze them in my fist, but we're wedged so closely together I can't get my arm between our bodies. Instead, I let my hands wander over two muscular thighs, marveling at how Blake's hair can feel thick and coarse under my palm while Jace's feels fine and soft.

Blake rocks against me before drawing back, his dick sliding lower on my stomach until he's far enough away that it hovers parallel to the ground, full and thick. Then he wraps his fist around it and gives a firm tug as he lines the head up to my clit.

He's barely touching me, the pressure so slight I'm not sure whether it's real or imagined. Either way, pleasure ripples through me so violently my knees start to buckle, and only Jace's body keeps me from sinking to the ground.

"Liked that, did you?" I feel Jace smile against my neck as his hand ghosts over my hip and settles on my ass. "Do it again, Blake."

Firmer this time, Blake rubs the head of his cock over my clit. The friction sends another jolt of ecstasy through my core as a cry mounts in my throat. Before I can utter a sound, another jolt hits me deep inside as Jace lightly tugs on the plug in my ass.

Engrossed by the hands and mouths laving me with attention, I'd almost forgotten it was there. As it slips away, I find myself clenching to keep it in place, straining to feel it rub against nerves deep inside I didn't even realize I could stimulate until now. I'm torn between chasing the friction on my clit and the pressure in my ass, both sensations so heavenly, I'm desperate to race to their conclusion.

"Slow down or she'll burst." Blake's eyes are glued to my pussy as he teases it with his fat head.

"Then we'll just have to make her come again, won't we?" Jace growls in my ear as he twists the plug while tugging it slowly. "Look what you're doing to Blake's cock."

Glancing down, I see the glistening head of Blake's dick circle my clit, and we moan in tandem.

"The things you do to me, Becca." Blake tilts my chin up and places a chaste kiss on my lips as he rubs his tip against me.

"The things she does to *us*," Jace rasps as his erection nudges my back. As if his words weren't heady enough, he presses the toy deeper, granting me the relief I was yearning for. *Temporarily.* Then he retracts it, achingly slow, and my head falls against his chest as I whimper my objection.

When I decided to take this step with the guys, it was partly to satisfy my own curiosity, and partly because I thought they'd enjoy it. They never asked, never even hinted at it, but a single girl has time to read some steamy romance, and what I read suggested guys like it when a woman takes two of them at once. I figured I'd test that for myself.

Getting ready for this was *interesting*. I almost chickened out a half dozen times, because my body wasn't happy about it at first. But in moving here, I made a conscious decision to challenge myself, professionally and personally. I wanted to break out of the shell I'd been living in. Though anal sex wasn't what I had in mind when I made that decision, it is technically a new challenge.

So, I pushed ahead. Literally. And it was... okay. Not phenomenal, but not entirely unpleasant, at first. Gradually, the foreign pressure became tolerable. Enjoyable even. But with Jace manipulating the toy while Blake teases my clit—I'm not sure I've ever been this aroused. It makes me anxious to have the real thing instead of a silicone substitute.

Back and forth, in and out, the two of them tease my aching nerves in a sensual torture that has me alternately gasping and groaning as I climb the precipice. Their tandem movements have me in a suspended euphoria, and I find myself straining for more friction. More pressure.

Anything that will drive me closer to the edge, and topple me into the blissful free fall that comes with release.

Then it's over. The pleasure gone, and the finish out of reach. Blake kisses my forehead and steps back as Jace withdraws the plug completely, leaving me cruelly empty. So much so, that if Jace wasn't holding me up from behind, I'm certain I'd have slumped to the floor.

I must wail, or frown, because a strong hand caresses my arms, my hair, my face. "Shh," Jace soothes. "We won't leave you wanting. Blake just had to grab condoms. Come lay down."

He guides me to the bed, holding me steady since my limbs are still shaky with raw desire. Once I'm settled on my back, he glides his fingers over my clit, soothing my frantic need. It takes the edge off just enough that my earlier panic subsides.

"Still with us, Becca?" Blake passes Jace a foil packet and bottle of lube, and once again hands leave my body. It leaves me aching, but the view of two gorgeous men kneeling beside me, rolling rubbers over their thick cocks, sates me enough that I don't growl my frustration.

"Yes," I sigh, admiring how their stomachs contract as they cover themselves.

"Think you can straddle me? Jace isn't as heavy as I am so you might be more comfortable with him on top." Blake strokes my hair away from my face, studying me with the most adorable look of concern. It'd probably make me melt if the need in my core didn't outweigh everything else right now.

Jace holds one hand while I brace the other on Blake's chest and swing my leg over his torso. Taking himself in hand, Blake lines up with my center, gritting his teeth as I sink onto his bulging length. The invasion is a welcome one, familiar, and my pussy clenches involuntarily as it tries to pull him deeper.

A contented breath passes through my lips when my pelvis nestles against his, our bodies fully joined. His warm hands glide up and down my thighs, stroking me reverently, as Jace cups my face in his hands.

"I'll be as gentle as I can, but if you don't like it tell me and I'll stop." His eyes drift closed as he leans forward, pressing his lips to mine in a tender, soulful kiss. It makes me feel treasured. And it forms a knot in my chest that takes all my willpower to swallow down before it turns to an all-out sob. *Don't go there, Becca. Not now.*

Jace grabs the lube and starts rubbing it over his cock as he moves behind me. "Lie down, beautiful. Put all your weight on Blake."

I stretch my legs out behind me as I lean forward, bracing my arms on either side of Blakes chest. A needy little whimper passes through my lips as the new position puts pressure on my clit. My hips start to move of their own accord, seeking out the friction Blake's body can provide, but his large hands blanketing my waist trap me in place.

"Not yet." He gives me a soft kiss. "Wait until Jace is ready."

Just then a drop of cool liquid slides down my ass, and my pussy clutches around Blake's cock. "Hurry up, Jace," he groans.

"Hold still." Tiny kisses feather along my spine, stopping just above my ass as firm hands spread me apart. "Breathe out while I push in, okay?"

I bob my head in agreement as pressure assaults my hole, forcing me to lock my jaw as my body tries to reject the intrusion. *Why is this happening? Didn't I prepare for this?*

"She's clenching. *Hard.*" Blake's voice is strained even though his eyes are soft.

Strong fingers massage my cheeks as Jace's soothing voice glides over me. "I'm bigger than the plug so it'll be hard at first. Just relax and breathe out."

I feel better knowing there's a reason this isn't going the way I envisioned, and with a heavy sigh I try to relax my muscles as I exhale. Though the initial push borders on painful, once the head of Jace's cock breeches my hole he moves easily, pressing deeper in a slow, steady thrust. Once again, the sensation of being stretched and filled sets my nerves on fire, erasing all discomfort as heat collects in my center.

"Damn." Blake's eyes roll back in his head as the tendons in his neck go taught. "I felt... Tell me that wasn't your dick I felt pressing against mine?"

"Did you like it?" Jace circles his hips slowly, setting off sparks of electricity deep inside my core as a strangled groan rumbles up Blake's throat.

"It was... I didn't know I'd feel you," Blake pants.

"We'll all feel each other." Jace swivels his hips again, brushing his thick head against a particularly sensitive spot. This time I'm the one who moans.

"Ready, Becca?" Soft lips kiss my shoulder. I nod again. "Blake and I are gonna move. Just relax and let us take care of you."

For reasons I can't explain, my arms and legs are too exhausted to function, so I give up trying to use them, letting my full weight sink against Blake's chest as they start to move.

Jace first, he withdraws slowly, leaving that empty feeling in his wake. Before I can mourn the loss, I feel him filling me again as Blake pulls back, leaving me despite the way my pussy contracts in an attempt to keep him in place. Back and forth, in and out, their cocks meeting in passing as they take turns filling me, all while I lay limply between them, savoring the friction and pressure building in my center.

Lost in a haze of bliss, I vaguely register whispered endearments. Baby. Beautiful. Honey. The occasional caress. A tender kiss. It's a stark contrast to the intrusions wreaking havoc on my body. Though being taken as a whole makes me feel both precious and wanton. How something so seemingly dirty can leave me feeling good I don't fully understand, I just know being here in this moment, between two men who both desire and respect me, feels right.

Pleasure mounts. Breathing becomes labored. Measured strokes push deeper, *harder*, as strong fingers grip my waist, my hips, holding me in place as they strain to bring us to the finish we'll all find buried in my core.

And then it's there. The precipice. Watching. Waiting. Beckoning me forward so it can carry me over the edge and consume me in its sated warmth. Thrust by determined thrust, I'm pushed to the brink, and then I'm falling. Spiraling. My throaty cries drowned out by the feral groans of the two men shuddering inside me as they follow me into the abyss.

Wracked with pleasure and senses on overdrive, I lie still as the aftershocks ripple through me. Too content to move let alone speak, I'm still foggy when strong arms tuck me between warm bodies, and soft lips pepper my skin. I barely make out the word *stay* murmured against my ear before a heavy, satiated sleep claims me.

When I wake the next morning, still cradled between their hard bodies and peaceful faces, my heart beats in an all too familiar pattern. I take in Blake's strong jaw, framed by a hint of stubble, then Jace's full lips, which I know are just as soft as the rest of his smooth skin. They're each sexy in their own way, not just in looks but personality. And they each sort of feel like home to me. *Shit. Is there a world where either of them would choose me, or where I don't have to choose between them?*

Chapter 25

Jace

I blink slowly as the mattress shifts, so subtly I think I'm imagining it, and let my eyes drift closed again, the pull of sleep too tempting to ignore. Then it moves again, a firmer jolt, and I turn my head to locate the disruption.

Like a thief in the night, Becca's stealing away, easing off the bed by degrees so she doesn't wake us. "What's the point in staying over if you're going to sneak out?" My voice is thick with sleep.

"I wasn't sneaking," she whispers. "I just didn't want to wake you both."

Rolling my head to the side, I see Blake lying on the other side of the void next to me. The one Becca's body filled a few seconds ago.

Stifling a yawn as he stretches his arms above his head he asks Becca, "Why are you getting dressed?"

"Brunch with the girls." She pulls a shirt over her head. "I have to go home to shower and then meet them at the restaurant."

She crawls onto the open space on the bed and leans over me, planting a quick kiss on my lips. "Call us later?" I ask as she does the same to Blake.

"Okay." She gives a little wave and slips out the door.

After a moment of silence, Blake asks, “Should we be worried that she bolted out of here?”

“I don’t think so. She kissed us goodbye.”

“True.” The mattress dips as he rolls to face me. “We didn’t talk to her about us.”

“I know.” I rub a hand over my face. “I wasn’t sure how to slow things down without hurting her feelings. She hasn’t taken charge like that before, and I didn’t want her to think I didn’t like it.”

“Trust me, I get it.” The hint of a smile passes over his lips as his eyes slowly close. “She was incredible last night. So brave even though she was nervous. So beautiful. I didn’t think it was possible to love her any more—or you—but after last night... We need to talk to her. Today. Do you have anything going on?”

“I need to talk to Axel, but Becca’s more important.”

“What do you have to talk to Axel about? Is something going on with the business?” There’s a hint of panic in his voice, like he’s expecting the ground to crumble beneath him since the foundation is still so fragile. I get that.

“Yes and no.” I roll to face him. “I’m still going to work with him, but I don’t want that to be my full-time gig.”

“You’re going back on the road?” He holds his breath.

“I’m actually hoping to be the resident expert for other riders who pass through. I could show people the best spots to film or do the filming myself. Summer and winter. If you’d show me those spots.”

“No more traveling?”

I grab his hand and hold it against my chest. “Not unless you’re with me. Becca, too.”

His hazel eyes gleam from beneath his disheveled hair. *God, he’s gorgeous when he’s happy.*

"You're right, you know." A smile plays on his lips. "This is going to work out."

"What makes you say that?" Since I'm usually the one trying to convince him of that, I'm curious where this optimism is coming from.

"She's falling in love with us." Blake's fingers trace the outline of my pec from underneath my palm.

"How can you tell?"

"Her eyes. The way they focus on us when we're together."

As the guy who makes a living watching people through a lens, I'm used to spotting these things myself, and I hadn't noticed.

"You mean while we're having sex?"

He shakes his head slightly. "That's not the only time, but that's how I noticed it. She looks at you the same way you look at me. The same way I'm pretty sure I look at both of you..." he trails off.

"What are you saying?" I squeeze his hand.

"I'm in. I mean out. No more secrets or half-truths. I want a life with you. Both of you. I don't want to just tell her we're bi, I want to tell her I love you. And I love her."

"You aren't afraid she isn't ready to hear that?"

"After last night..." He shakes his head firmly. "No."

"You're good with all of it, then? Not just admitting you like men and women but telling people you're *dating* a man and a woman. Are you ready for that?"

"Are you?" he asks defensively.

"I didn't grow up here. I don't have roots here. You do." I brush a wayward lock of hair away from his face. "You know I'm all in, but people here don't know me from anyone. It won't bother me if they don't approve of my lifestyle."

"Sorry." He exhales heavily. "I didn't mean to get defensive. It's just that I *am* ready. And yeah, I know it's possible that some people will take issue with it, and of course that'll hurt. But not as much as missing out on a life with you and Becca. I love you."

Up until the other day, no one—guy or girl—had said that to me before. Now that I've heard it, I'm not sure I'll ever get tired of it.

"I love you, too."

Leaning forward, I press my lips to Blake's, a soft, gentle confirmation that my life is bound to his from here forward. It's not enough.

We've barely touched since Becca came into the picture, and while I wouldn't trade our time with her for anything, I can't deny that I've missed being able to taste him freely. Tilting my head to the side I coax his lips apart, straining to get our mouths as close as possible.

"More," he groans into me.

Scooting closer, I press our dicks together and wrap my hand around them, stroking rhythmically as our tongues wrestle for dominance. It's not rough, though not gentle either. His morning shadow scrapes across my skin as his needy lips devour mine, which sets my body on fire.

Breaking away, I rub my jaw against his. "I love the way your stubble feels on my skin."

"I love the way your cock feels next to mine," he growls.

"Me, too." I contract my hand as I slide it over us. "Need you, Blake. I need to be inside you."

He rolls away and retrieves the lube from the nightstand, tossing it to me as he positions himself on his hands and knees.

"Condom," I grunt as my slippery fingers play with his hole.

"We used them all last night." He looks at me over his shoulder. "And I want you bare."

The air gets sucked out of my lungs as my hand stills against his opening, the magnitude of his words seeping into my soul.

"On your back," I say softly, pulling away to give him room to flip over. "I want to see you while I'm inside you."

Our eyes meet and lock, an unspoken promise passing between us. Then he shifts so he's lying on his back, pulling his knees to his chest as he opens himself to me.

Though we done this before—not just sex but sex in this position—there's something symbolic about it today. He's opening himself to me completely, physically and emotionally, which makes this moment more meaningful than any of the other times we've come together. This is the start of a new chapter for both of us. One he's willingly embracing after years of hesitation and uncertainty, and I love him for it.

Coating my dick with the lube I press gently forward, holding my breath until I'm fully seated. When we're joined completely, I find Blake's eyes and exhale as I start to thrust, holding his gaze in mine.

The slide of his skin on mine, the pressure of his walls contracting around me is the most delicious friction, begging me to move faster. Harder. But I want to savor this. Savor him.

Leaning forward I pin his arms to the bed above him, linking our fingers together. Face to face, lips mere inches apart, I plead. "Tell me again."

"I love you."

"Again." I thrust, slow and deep.

"I love you."

A loud gasp has both our heads turning toward the door to find Becca, mouth hanging open, wide eyes glued on our naked bodies. Our *joined* naked bodies.

I never understood the expression *'time stands still'* until this moment, where it does in fact seem to freeze as we all process what we're seeing. Then Becca's jaw starts to move, her voice only coming out after several false starts.

"My... I forgot my..." She blinks and spins around, disappearing from sight. Searing hot pain ripples through my chest and settles in my gut, like a knife ripping out my soul and leaving me just a hollow shell. *Fuck*! Without taking a moment to question my actions I pull out of Blake and race after her.

"Wait," I cry. "Becca, wait."

"Sorry. I'm sorry." She races toward the door. "I shouldn't have come in without knocking."

Catching her by the arm I spin her around to face me. "You belong here. You don't have to knock."

She gives me a once over, gesturing to my still hard cock. "Clearly, that's not true."

Blake comes running into the room clad only in his boxers, holding a pair to out to me. Instead of taking them, I wrap both hands around Becca's arms. Pulse throbbing in my chest, I strain to keep my voice level. "It is true, honey. You belong right here. *With* us."

She lifts her arm at the elbow, trying to point to Blake. "He just said he loves you. That's a pretty clear sign that I... Oh wow." She blinks rapidly, eyes darting between us. "How did I not see this before?"

"See what?" Blake's sun-kissed skin looks pasty, his body so still I almost wonder if he's breathing.

"You weren't afraid to touch him." She gapes at me. "I just thought... Oh God, that wasn't to turn me on it was... I was just... *A cover?* A way to keep people from suspecting you're gay? Well, it worked. Even I didn't suspect anything until this morning." She spins away from my grasp and throws open the front door.

"That's not what this is," I call after her.

Blake snaps out of his stupor, barreling outside behind her with me hot on his heels. "You don't understand, let us explain."

"Please, Becca," I plead. "You've got the wrong idea. Come back inside."

"What did I get wrong?" She spins to face us so fast I crash into Blake when he stops short. "Are you two not together?"

Blake's eyes dart to mine. "We are, but..."

A shrill cry cuts him off, and the three of us look to the street to find an older couple walking their dog, staring at us with jaws hanging open.

"Hi Jim. Hey Teri." Blake waves awkwardly. Stunned, I start to mimic him, but a piercing pain in my side stops me from lifting my arm. I cut a glare toward Blake, whose lips are set in a firm line as he jerks his head to the front door.

"What?" I hiss.

His eyes drop down, and when I follow his gaze realization hits. I'm still naked, my half-hard dick pointing lamely toward Becca. *Screw it.* She's more important than my dignity.

"Becca, please." I try again as the couple staggers away, darting glances over their shoulders as they go. "You don't know the whole story. Come inside so we can explain."

She gives a subtle but firm shake of her head as a lone tear slides down her face, and my heart fractures inside my chest. "I know I'm the third wheel, that's enough. I'm late." She stalks to her car and locks herself inside, backing out in a rush as Blake and I watch in pained silence.

Please let this be a bad dream.

As her car disappears around the corner, my hope plummets. Deflated, I head inside and grab the boxers from where Blake dropped them on the floor. By the time he joins me on the couch, I'm decent, but nowhere near okay.

"It's futile to think maybe she'll come back, isn't it?" he asks softly.

"I don't know." I rub my hand over my face, as if that might hold my head together. "She seems determined to believe she's some sort of side piece. Fuck! That couldn't have gone any worse."

"Actually, it can." He exhales heavily.

"What? How?"

Blake leans forward, resting his elbows on his knees as he wrings his hands together and shoots nervous glances my way. "Jim and Teri saw us."

"Who the fuck are Jim and Teri?"

"They live one block over. Teri runs the bookshop in town, which means the secret's out."

I reach over and grab the hand closest to me, hoping it calms him. I hope it calms me down, too. "It was coming out anyway, wasn't it?"

"Yeah." His head falls to his chest. "But I wanted it to come from me."

"I'm sorry." Being outed by others is a fear second only to having those closest to you reject who you are. Despite how badly we screwed this up, he doesn't deserve that.

"It's not your fault." Blake squeezes my fingers, though there's no reassurance behind the gesture. *Is he already giving up?* "I should have come out the moment you moved in, before Becca was even involved. Maybe it would've prevented all this."

He's not wrong—not entirely—but I can't blame him.

"And maybe it would've kept her from getting involved with us at all. Besides, I agreed to keep it quiet, which makes this just as much my fault." I rub the lingering ache in my chest, trying to keep my shit together.

A shrill bell pierces the air, and Blake drops my hand to reach for his phone, sitting on the coffee table where he left it last night. His shoulders slump as he hits accept.

"Hey, Mom... That didn't take long. Teri must have called you as soon as she walked in the door..."

His eyes fall shut as he takes a shaky breath

"There's a perfectly good explanation... No, I'm not on drugs."

He pinches the bridge of his nose.

"My roommate isn't, either. He's..." Blake holds his breath as muffled sounds come from near his ear.

"He wasn't flashing them on purpose... No, no one was cheating on anyone. Look." Blake exhales heavily, and I take his hand again, squeezing it firmly in mine. "This isn't how I wanted to tell you, but... No, I'm not sick. Mom, listen."

Lifting his eyes to mine, Blake holds my gaze as he bares his soul. "My roommate, Jace... He's more than just my roommate. He's my boyfriend. And the girl who was here this morning... She's our girlfriend. Or we'd like her to be..."

I know Blake's world is in a tailspin right now, but I've never been so in awe of another person, and my best friend is a pro dirt biker with a couple of world titles under his belt. I mouth the words *I love you*, and the corner of his lip lifts in a relieved yet forlorn sort of way.

"I'm bisexual, Mom," he says. "And I recently found a man—and a woman—I'd like to spend my life with... Yes, the same woman Teri saw leaving this morning... I didn't do a very good job of explaining what she meant to me."

I squeeze Blake's hand and give a slight shake of my head. "*We* didn't do a good job explaining what she means to *us*," he amends, and I nod. Then his jaw falls open.

"Say that again." He puts the phone on speaker.

"Relationships with two people can be tough, I can't imagine the confusion with three." A soft, gentle voice echoes from the speaker as Blake's hazel eyes meet mine, wide with surprise.

"You uh, seem to be taking this pretty well," he stutters.

"That's because it's not a surprise."

"You knew?" His brow furrows in a mixture of confusion and shock.

"I had my suspicions when your superhero phase was more about the actors playing the heroes than the powers they had. And your dad said you once saw a girl so pretty you about snapped your neck trying to get another look at her. I admit I wasn't expecting you to fall for two people at once, but as long as they make you happy then I'm happy for you. When do I get to meet them?"

His eyes look a little glassy as he blinks them in rapid succession. "As soon as Jace and I get our girl back."

Chapter 26

Blake

I hang up the phone and give my head a shake to clear it. "I guess high school me wasn't as good at pretending that I didn't notice guys as I thought I was."

"Captain America was your favorite, wasn't he? I can see a little boy scout underneath the rugged bike guy thing you've got going on." For the first time since Becca left, he almost smiles. "And you've got his square jaw underneath that stubble."

"You think I look like Chris Evans?" That almost makes me smile myself. Almost. "I can't complain about that. I don't think I've got a boy scout quality, though. Not after the way I handled things."

I love Jace for wanting to share the blame, but when it comes down to it *I'm* the one who was reluctant to come out, so *I'm* the one that may have just cost us our shot at happiness with Becca. Maybe even with the two of us.

We may have made promises to each other about staying together regardless of what happened with her, but that was before we got glimpses of how epic things could be with the three of us. I can't unsee how perfect that future looked, so even if losing her doesn't tear Jace and I apart, there will always be a void where Becca should be.

Please let us be able to fix this.

"We both screwed up. Instead of getting hung up on that, let's figure out how to fix it." Jace chews on his lip for a moment before nudging me with an elbow. "Think your mom would have any ideas?"

That snaps me out of my funk. "My *Mom*? Why the hell do you think she'd have any ideas?"

"She made that comment about relationships being hard." He lifts a shoulder like that explains everything.

"Would you ask your mom for advice about how you and your boyfriend could win back your girlfriend?"

He runs a hand through his hair. "Yeah, okay. Bad idea. Think maybe one of the guys would know what to do? I mean, Finn and Cade are *married*. They've gotta have some good advice."

Though Jace isn't acting jittery, the fact that he's tossing out random, *ridiculous* ideas tells me his outer calm is an act, probably for my benefit. *Shit*. If he's worried then...

The doorbell has us looking at each other expectantly for a split second before we launch off the couch and scramble for the door, our arms and legs a tangle of limbs as we claw over one another to get there with single-minded focus. *Please let it be her.*

I throw open the door to find Axel on the threshold, an uncharacteristic frown on his face. He looks over each of us head to toe before shoving his way inside "Get dressed. We've gotta talk."

Jace and I exchange a nervous glance before trailing him into the living room.

"What are you doing here?" Jace plays casual.

Axel spins abruptly, stopping us in our tracks. "Lennon told me Becca canceled on brunch. Apparently, she's not feeling so hot, although she sounded more depressed than sick. Like she'd been crying. Lennon thought you two would like to know.

"Why us? What does Lennon know." Jace's voice is eerily level, his stiff arms evidence that he's holding onto control by a thread.

Axel crosses his arms in front of his chest, though he's too nice a guy to look truly intimidating. Just like a disappointed older brother. That's almost worse. "Pretty much everything."

"What the fuck, man?" Jace explodes. "I told you about the three of us in confidence."

"Yeah, well, I was worried you'd get hurt with all your secrets, but you wouldn't listen to me. So, I talked to Lennon." He twists to face me. "She's the only one, though. You're friends with her, you know she'd never say anything."

Jace glances to me and I nod to reassure him. "Lennon's solid." Turning to Axel I add, "I wish you hadn't told her before I did, though. Like you said, I'm friends with her."

Axel has the decency to duck his head as he replies. "Fair enough. But she might be able to save your asses, so it's a good thing she's in the know."

"Save our asses?" Jace interrupts. "What are you talking about?"

"My guess is Becca found out about the two of you before you had a chance to come clean on your own. Right?" Axel prompts.

Jace and I share a guilty look, which Axel doesn't miss.

"Fuck." Axel wheels on Jace. "You didn't even ask if she's into this lifestyle, did you? So, in her mind, the two of you are the couple and she's the extra spice on the side."

My hands ball into fists at my side. "Don't talk about her like that."

"You two are who I'm criticizing, not her." Axel points at each of us in turn. "I told him weeks ago," he jerks his head at Jace, "that this would blow up in your faces, and here we are. I'm not part of this trio but even I know more about it than she does. How do you think that makes her feel? Embarrassed? Ashamed? Like she doesn't mean enough to know the truth?"

"How is this helping?" Jace barks as I sink onto the couch, my stomach feeling like it's about to lose contents it doesn't have. *This is so bad.* "We get it, we fucked up," Jace continues. "Telling us that won't fix shit."

"I'm trying to help you figure out how to get her back." Axel throws his arms in the air like he's done with us. "Maybe if you understand where she's coming from, you guys can fix it. Put yourself in her shoes, what would you want to hear? And don't say sorry, that's not good enough."

Jace glares at his best friend, panting with barely contained rage. "Jesus, dude. Get yourself a girlfriend and suddenly you're a fucking expert? What makes you think you're right?"

"This isn't my advice, it's Lennon's. She said Becca needs to know *why* you screwed up. Even if your logic is fucked up, knowing where you're coming from is the only thing that *might* make her forgive you."

Jace's nostrils flare, but he doesn't object to Axel's words. I can't either.

"He's right," I admit. "What we saw as easing her into things she probably sees as toying with her. And telling her how we feel won't solve anything. She won't forgive us for keeping secrets until she understands *why* we did it. That our intentions were good even if our actions were shit."

"And how do we do that?" Jace asks. "She's not coming back over, how do we get her to listen to us?"

"Knock on her door and ask to talk to her." Axel shrugs, as if it's that simple. *I guess Lennon didn't advise him on this part.*

"What if she doesn't want to talk?" Jace's eyes fall shut as he rubs his forehead.

"I can ask Carter to give us a key to her room?" I suggest, feeling a twinge of hope for the first time since she walked out.

"Let me stop you there." Axel shakes his head at me. "A, that's technically breaking in, so no. B, shouldn't you be a little more discreet than involving your boss in this little triangle? After all, if you were so concerned about whether she'd be on board with this lifestyle it's not fair to put her in it without her permission."

"Shit, I know." I scrub a hand over my face. *I'm fucking losing it.* "I'm just freaking out about not being able to fix this."

"I hear you. I felt the same way when I thought I'd fucked up with Lennon. But you can't just march in there and give her some bullshit line about trying to protect her or breaking the news gently. I know you think that's what you were doing." He pins Jace with a look that says, *don't even try to object.* "Although the truth is, you were both so busy thinking about what you wanted you forgot to think about what she might want."

"Fuck," I groan, letting my head fall back against the couch cushions. "She's never gonna forgive us."

"She might. Just give her some time and..."

"Screw that," Jace interrupts Axel. "The longer we go without trying to fix it the longer she has to convince herself this is a mistake. I won't take that chance."

"Me, either." I fly off the couch, ready, as Jace's steely resolve gives me another burst of hope.

"Stop." Axel's booming voice freezes us both halfway to the front door. "Whatever groveling you two have to do is gonna go a whole lot better if you're dressed."

Jace and I look at each other, before looking down at ourselves. Then we speed walk to the bedroom to find clothes.

Chapter 27

Becca

Tears make my vision cloudy as I stumble into my apartment, but I'm too stubborn to let them fall. Not outside these four walls where anyone could see them.

I'm such a fool.

I want to call Liz and cry my heart out, but don't feel like hearing the *I told you so* speech, especially because when she said someone would get hurt, I'm pretty sure we assumed it would be one of the guys, not me. Yet here I am, alone and *heartbroken*. Flopping on the couch, I bury my head in a throw pillow.

It was futile to think I could sleep with them and not develop feelings. Some part of me knew that all along, yet I did it anyway. I let myself believe it was strictly curiosity, having a good time, but the truth is I wanted more time with both Blake and Jace than the one night I'd had with each, and I convinced myself I could have that without consequences because I *wanted* to.

Now, having ignored my common sense, I'm right back where I started when I got here. Worse, because instead of looking forward to a new job and a new town, I'm dreading having to face both. This mistake will be staring me in the face at every turn, and there's nowhere to hide.

Hiding.

Hiding in plain sight is more like it. How did I not see there was something between them? Was the idea of them being so comfortable during sex such a turn on that I didn't question it. Or maybe I just didn't want to contemplate the answer. But after seeing them together, hearing them confess their feelings, I feel like a fool for missing the obvious. And to top off my embarrassment, they're actually beautiful together. The way they were looking into each other's eyes, like they were the only two people in existence. It made my heart swell even as it started to ache.

Somehow in this mess I'd been foolish enough to believe they looked at me like that too. Clearly, that was a figment of my imagination. They were probably looking at each other and I got in the way. Claimed those looks as my own instead of something they meant for each other.

The velvety pillow muffles my scream.

I've never been so humiliated. Or felt so alone. Not even Brian left me feeling this empty. At least he cheated on me behind my back instead of bringing me into his sordid affairs. And he never went out of his way to make me feel cherished, lulling me into a false sense of affection.

When am I going to learn?

There was never going to be a happy ending here. I should be grateful it's over now, instead of months or years down the road, when my heart was well and truly theirs. *Oh, who am I kidding? It's already theirs.*

I drag my wrist across my face, wiping away the tears and snot before they trickle to my lip.

No wonder my relationships fail. For a moment there, I actually wondered if I could have them both. *Stupid.* And as if that wasn't bad enough, I'm pretty sure the whole town is about to realize exactly what—whom—I've been doing since I got here. *Brilliant.*

A sharp rap on the door interrupts my pity party, and I cautiously sit up, wondering if that knock was real or imagined since no one has ever come by before. Then it sounds again, more urgent this time, and a strained voice seeps through the cracks.

"Becca? We're here, and we only need a minute. Please, will you open the door?"

I'm not ready to face them. Not with puffy eyes, a runny nose, and enough humiliation to make my face even more pink than my hair. But living in employee housing means this place is full of employees—my co-workers—who absolutely do not need to know the depths of my depravity or delusions.

Moving swiftly to the door, I open it just wide enough that they don't have to shout through it.

"Oh, thank God," Blake exhales. "We know you might not be ready to hear it, but when you are, there's a lot we have to say." He licks his lips nervously. "About the three of us."

Next to him, Jace shuffles from one foot to the other. "We just needed you to know that. So, please, before you tell us to fuck off, please let us tell you everything. When you're ready."

I've never seen either of them so distressed before, and despite the fact that they deserve to grovel for *a lot* longer, my soft heart hates seeing them this way, even after what they did. I open the door wide enough for them to pass through, and with a startled glance at each other, they do.

Closing the door, I spin to find Jace's hands shoved awkwardly in his pockets, while Blake wrings his in front of him. Keeping my face carefully blank, I walk to the couch and sit down, each of them taking a seat next to me.

Blake reaches for me but freezes his arm before he can make contact, dropping his elbows to his knees and twisting his fingers together. I arch my eyebrow, waiting.

"I uh..." he starts. "Until this morning I've been in the closet. No one but Jace knew I'm bisexual. It's not something I'm ashamed of, although I was willing to take the easy way out by not saying anything until I met the person I wanted to spend my life with." His eyes dart briefly to Jace, I assume since I heard them confessing their love earlier, before coming to rest on me.

Blake licks his lips and continues. "If that person was a woman, I'd never have to say anything, and if it was a man I'd come out. Looking back I can see how that wasn't fair to the people I care about, but I spent years believing that was the best solution, so I didn't question it. And I especially didn't question whether more than one person could be right for me."

Is he trying to justify sleeping with me despite loving Jace?

"I've been out for a long time." Jace bounces his leg as his gaze darts from it to me. "Out as bi, I mean, and I was always pretty open to the idea that I might one day find a man—and a woman—I wanted to be with. It's not something I sought out, but if I let myself daydream about my future that's what it looked like. I connected with Blake right away, and I moved here knowing he could be that man. Wanted him to be, actually." Jace shoots Blake a sheepish smile before focusing his gaze on me.

I spin to see Blake's reaction and find him nodding solemnly. "Great. You two are in love. Is that supposed to make me feel better about sleeping with you? You weren't cheating on each other or anything since you were both there?"

"No, it's..." Jace scrubs a hand down his face. "Let me finish. I found Blake, and things were going really good. Great actually. Then you got here, and suddenly that future daydream I'd always had in the back of my mind started to feel like it could be real. But I didn't know how to tell you I wanted Blake much less the two of you together, and since we'd both already had a sexual relationship with you, that seemed like a good place to start."

"But sex was only supposed to be the way we approached wanting more, because we thought asking you to date both of us at once might send you running the other direction." Blake jumps in. "We never meant to imply that's all we wanted."

So, sex was a way to lead into me being their girlfriend?

It pains me to admit, but their logic isn't as backward as it sounds. If they led with dating, I would've scoffed and told them they were crazy. By leading with sex, they made things casual enough to be comfortable, and opened the door for my feelings to grow. However, understanding their motives doesn't mean I agree with them. They still manipulated me, however innocent their intentions may have been in their minds. They used sex to drive my feelings and hid the fact that they were together all along. Even though I was starting to wonder if there was a way I could avoid having to choose between them, learning that I'm the *add on* to their couple is a hard pill to swallow.

Blake runs a hand through his already ruffled hair. "We should have told you this sooner, and it's my fault we didn't."

"Ours," Jace interrupts.

"You agreed to it, but I'm the one who was holding out." Blake turns his guilty gaze to me. "You're new to town, you've got a new job, and I know those things are challenging enough without adding us to the mix." He draws a line between he and Jace. "I wasn't sure you'd jump at the chance to go public about dating two guys. And selfishly, that let me hide who I am a little longer, while I tried to wrap my head around my feelings."

"What's there to wrap your head around? I heard you say you love Jace."

"I do. But he's not the only one." The corner of Blake's lip tips up in a bashful smile.

"That's what we're trying to tell you, honey." Jace cups his hand around my neck and strokes my cheek. "We love you, too. Blake and I may have started out as a couple, but once we discovered that we'd both been with you, and we both felt drawn to you the same way we did to each other, we knew we wouldn't be complete without you. We just didn't know how to express what you mean to us, and we let sex be the cop out until we thought you were ready to hear the truth."

"You thought I'd object to the two of you being together?" My heart sinks. *When did I give them the impression I don't approve of gay—bi—men?*

"We thought we might scare you off if we told you how serious we are about you." Jace reaches for my hand, and though I'm still leery of what they're saying, I let him take it. "Our feelings for you were pretty intense right from the start. And by the start I don't mean when you moved here, I mean when we first met you."

"That was..." My mouth falls open as I stare at Jace, dumbfounded.

"A year ago. Yeah." I swear his cheeks turn pink with that admission. "Blake's the fate guy, but having the two of you here—the only two people I'd ever wanted to make something real with—that's a sign even I couldn't ignore. The three of us...I want it more than anything."

"So, you're saying I'm not the side piece in your..." I wave my hand around as I search for the word I want. "Couple?"

"You're the piece that holds us together," Blake says softly. "Or, we want you to be."

I open and shut my mouth, then open and shut it again. "Can that really work? *Three people*?" I may have been fantasizing about that a little this morning since I'd developed feelings for both men, and couldn't imagine having to choose between them. But I don't think I was taking that fantasy seriously. I mean... *three people?*

"It was working, wasn't it?" Blake shrugs sheepishly. "The three of us compliment each other. You and Jace are brave where I'm practical, you and I are social where he's independent, and he and I can be idiots where you're smart. The fact that we're having this conversation is proof."

I press my lips together to contain my grin—Blake's self-deprecating humor really is charming—though he's making this sound much simpler than it is. Things may have been working in the bedroom, but what happens when we step out of it? Will we be shunned by the town? Will my job be in jeopardy? Will my sister accept or even tolerate my lifestyle?

"Plus," Jace continues before I can finish my thoughts, "we all have an adventurous side that likes to explore and soak up the outdoors. Plenty of two-person couples don't fit together as well as the three of us do."

My history with Brian is evidence of that. Still, what sounds good in theory can't be this easy in practice. Can it?

"Becca," Jace starts, "Blake and I love each other, and we love you. The question is, do you think you could love us?"

Putting aside the external factors—my job and my reputation—that I should consider, I can honestly say I have feelings for both men. Feelings that originated from the time I met each of them, and which grew over these past several weeks, enough so that I was starting to panic over how to navigate them without hurting anyone.

Regardless of how unconventional this is, both Blake and Jace have touched my spirit in a way no one else has, simply by accepting me for who I am. I've never felt inadequate with them, never doubted my own mind. I can truly be myself with them, something I've rarely felt with anyone else, even Liz, who despite being my biggest supporter never quite got me the way Blake and Jace do. Is that love? It's more than I ever felt for Brian, who I did think I loved, so yeah. It may make me slightly crazy, but I do think I can love them both. I'm halfway there already.

"Yes."

The word barely passes through my lips before Jace's are on me, soft and savoring. Then Blake tilts my chin toward him and takes his turn, showing me the depth of the feelings in his heart. Back and forth, they take turns worshiping me with their mouths; confessing their regrets, begging forgiveness, and pledging their love. It's poignant, and emotional, and touches my very soul. It's also them and me, not the three of us.

Pulling back, I cup each of their faces in my palm. "Now you two."

Blake licks his lips with a shaky breath as Jace wraps a hand around his neck. Then their lips meet, right in front of my eyes, and a soft moan rumbles from Blake's throat. Their eyes are delicately shut, tongues subtly meeting between barely parted lips, and it's so beautiful I swear my eyes get a little misty.

Then I realize my eyes aren't the only place I'm wet.

During a few of our encounters, Jace touched Blake, and I got a tiny thrill when I saw it. This kiss is even hotter, which has me wondering what else between them might turn me on. In fact, I'm pretty sure if shock hadn't taken over earlier today, I'd have enjoyed watching them screw each other.

I must gulp or lick my lips or do something to give away the direction of my thoughts, because suddenly they're both staring at me with a mix of curiosity and hunger that has me rubbing my thighs together.

"Sorta looks like she's enjoying this little show, doesn't it?" Jace's mouth lifts in a lascivious smile.

"Something you want to tell us, Becca?" Blake's grin rivals Jace's.

Oh Boy. *I want to see you rub your cocks together, I want to see you suck each other off, I want to watch you fuck.* Lewd fantasies bombard me faster than I knew I could conjure them, the depth of my curiosity apparently bottomless. Instead, I trap my lips between my teeth and shake my head with wide, guilty eyes. Eyes that wander downward of their own accord.

"I think someone wants a better view." Jace stands up and strips off his shirt before reaching for the button on his pants.

Blake follows suit, watching me with a sly gaze. "When I came home yesterday and saw you and Jace...Watching your lovers fuck is one of the most beautiful things I've ever seen. Also, the hottest. Is that what you want? To watch us?"

I'm not embarrassed to say that per se, this is just all so new I'm not sure how to put my thoughts into words yet. "Maybe?" I gnaw on my lip, glancing bashfully between them.

As is normal—probably since he's the most experienced of all of us—Jace takes charge. Fully naked, he takes a step forward and drags the length of his rigid cock along Blake's, letting out a contented sigh when they make contact.

Back and forth, their dicks grind against each other as they rock their hips, the swollen flesh growing firmer with the ebb and flow of their sensual dance. Blake rests a large hand on Jace's waist, whether for balance or just to satisfy the need to touch him I'm not sure, but his movements seem to speed up, and both their tips start to glisten with tiny beads of precum.

Their eyes track from their faces to their cocks, over to me, and back, both of them absorbing every detail.

The way they move together.

The way I watch them.

The way we all start breathing heavily.

Jace is strangely silent, offering no instruction as their bodies come together. Then Blake reaches between Jace's legs and cups his heavy balls in his hand, massaging them with his fingers. "This is Jace's fantasy come true, Becca. The three of us together—no barriers. No secrets." Jace's head falls back as Blake teases him with his hands and his dick. "It's making him so hard."

The evidence of that is proudly displayed before me, and despite loving the image of the two of them I'm suddenly impatient to join in. Leaning forward, mouth open, my tongue darts out to lick across Jace's tip. Then Blake's.

By some unspoken agreement they angle their bodies toward me, taking turns offering me their cocks. With each pass one rubs the head of his dick along the other's length into my waiting mouth, then pulls back to make room for the other. I lick and suck and even kiss the firm, smooth skin that strains toward me, loving the way their hooded eyes track the way the three of us move together.

Pressing my thighs together, I scoot forward, eager to explore this newfound dynamic. My excitement doesn't go unnoticed.

"Look at how she squirms. This is turning her on," Jace growls.

"What now, Becca?" Blake strokes my cheek as he rubs his swollen head over my tongue. "Tell us what you want next."

Jace faces Blake and grips them both in his hand, stroking slowly as they watch me intently. Waiting.

"Um," I swallow audibly as my mind runs through the possibilities.

Despite running away earlier, the glimpse I had of the two of them together has been playing on repeat all day. Part of that is because they were so clearly in tune with one another, but part of it is that I found it so erotic. The desperation in their breathing, the groans of pleasure rumbling from their throats, their declarations of love. I wasn't willing to admit it when anger and hurt blinded me, but that was one of the hottest things I've ever witnessed, and instead of averting my gaze like I did before I want to look my fill this time.

"I want to watch. What you were doing this morning." I can't bring myself to say it, not because it offends me or I'm embarrassed, but because I'm not sure what to call it. Fucking seems too vulgar, and making love is... Well, it might be accurate, although I don't want to presume since the moment wasn't meant for me.

Wasn't meant for me. That thought isn't as harsh now as it was this morning. Maybe it should be—they were dishonest after all—but at least now I can appreciate why they felt they had to be, and I can respect rather than resent their feelings for each other. That, as Blake indicated, makes watching the two of them express those feelings a beautiful thing instead of a horrific one. And a massive turn on.

"Take us to your bedroom, then." Jace lets go of their cocks and holds his hand out to me so he can help me off the couch.

I lead them to my room on shaky limbs, my heart beating erratically in my chest. *I can't believe this is happening.*

"Lie down, Blake. Ass by the edge of the bed," Jace commands. As Blake follows his instructions, Jace turns to me and gives me a tender kiss. "I'm gonna need your help, beautiful."

"Wha...what do you mean?" I stammer.

"I didn't come prepared, and I'll hurt him if I go dry." When I offer no response, he continues, thumb stroking gently over my parted lips. "I need your mouth, Becca. Or your pussy."

Heat rushes to my cheeks as understanding dawns, and moisture floods my panties. This morning I couldn't have imagined that sentence turning me on, but now... *Holy shit*. My tongue darts out to lick my lips, swiping along Jace's thumb in the process. A soft groan slips from his throat.

"On the bed," he growls.

Shedding my clothes, I climb on the bed next to Blake, scooting to the edge, knees up, just like he is. As he leans in to kiss me warm fingers spread me open, and cool air drifts over my clit. Then Jace's cock slides along my folds.

I whimper at the contact, reveling in the pleasure and wanting more. He doesn't offer it. Slow and steady, he rubs his cock between my legs, coating it in my arousal, all while Blake's lips savor mine. Gentle. Indulgent. His mouth probes mine delicately, as if he wants to make this moment linger forever. My body hums with the knowledge that that's exactly what this could be the start of. Forever.

Lost in the press of Blake's lips against mine, I barely register the absence of Jace's rigid length between my legs. Then Blake tenses, a sated growl reverberating in his throat, and I realize Jace has filled him.

Overwhelmed with curiosity, I pull my mouth from Blake's and kneel beside him. His muscled frame shifts on the mattress as Jace thrusts forward, both men groaning as they come together fully.

They hold still for a moment before Jace starts to move, his lean stomach contracting as he swivels his hips. Teeth clenched in concentration, his eyes rake over me, then Blake, as he presses deep inside Blake's body with slow, measured thrusts. A thin sheen of sweat gathers on his torso with the strain of going slow written in the pained expression on his face. But he holds steady, exaggerating each stroke so I can see every last inch of him as he moves.

Shifting my gaze to Blake, I notice his expression mirrors Jace's. Primed yet not sated, his hips lift to meet Jace's as if begging him to go deeper. Push harder. Though, he too, moves slowly, prolonging each thrust.

My eyes skirt down over his chest, down his stomach, coming to rest on the thick cock standing at attention. "Touch him," Jace orders.

I wrap my hand around Blake's swollen length, squeezing as tight as I dare. "*Oh Damn.*" Blake rewards me with a strangled moan.

"Move with me," Jace instructs, his heated, dark eyes commanding me to match his pace.

Together, we pleasure Blake, and Jace bottoms out each time I stroke down to Blake's root. His cock twitches in my hand, and I squeeze harder, rubbing my finger over the slick tip. His eyes roll back in his head as it dips into the mattress, and my chest swells with pride knowing Jace and I *together* are driving him mad.

The power we have over Blake's pleasure is intoxicating. Screw fierce flamingos, it makes me feel like the goddess I never believed I could be, and drives me to grip him a little tighter, tug a little faster, to see how high we can take him. It also gets me positively *dripping*, and I shift my legs to sate my own gathering need.

"He's ready for you. If you want him." Jace pulls my hand off Blake's dick as he plunges hard and deep, leaning forward to taste Blake's parted lips. Then he stands straight, still buried in Blake's ass, and gestures for me to sit on his stiff cock.

Taking Jace's hand for balance, I swing my leg over Blake's torso, my back to his face, and sink onto his swollen length. Jace holds still until I'm seated, nipping at my bottom lip while he waits for me to adjust.

My breathy sigh must be the sign he's looking for—no sooner does it pass my lips than he starts to pump in earnest, his pelvis brushing against my clit with each pass.

Blake's strong hands wrap around my waist, anchoring me to him, though Jace's relentless thrusts spear him deeper and deeper inside, teasing my heightened nerves.

Jace leans his head against mine, lips hovering together as we pant. It's desperate. Frantic. Yet, so much more intimate and erotic than an actual kiss. *I love it.*

Wrapping one hand around his neck, I trace the sinewy muscles of his chest with the other, letting my fingers drift down until they find the soft curls that frame his dick. Delving lower, I rub his base, my fingers getting trapped between his body and Blake's with each thrust, the back of my hand rubbing against my clit in the process.

"I'm close, Becca. He's close," Jace mutters against my lips as he drives Blake deep within my core. "Come with us."

I don't know if it's his plea or my own desire that makes me comply, but suddenly the telltale prickle of bliss is within reach, and my body starts to soar. Warmth radiates from my center, spearing down to my toes and out to my fingertips, as my pussy starts to contract. Faintly at first, the intensity grows as Blake's cock nudges deep within me, my walls flexing and contracting of their own accord as my release consumes me.

Erotic cries assault my senses. Between my own heartbeat and the animalistic growls of the men, the sounds reverberate through me like the heavy bass of a guitar, shaking my whole body. Spent, I can do little more than cling to Jace as I try to stay upright while the tremors flow through me and fade to nothingness, like the ripples from a rock skipping across the water.

Gradually, the dense thudding in my ears is replaced by heavy breathing, the soothing caress of Blake's hands running over my waist. Fingers cramping from their strangled hold on Jace, I tentatively flex them to bring them back to life as I lift off Blake, hoping my shaky legs can support my weight.

Two sets of hands help me to the bed, where the three of us collapse. Blake and Jace thread their fingers together and rest them on my stomach, anchoring us together as we wait for our bodies to recover. It's in this moment, right now, that I know committing to them both is the right choice. That we really are meant to be.

"I hate to kill the mood." Blake rolls to his back and slings a forearm over his head. "But we haven't talked about the bigger picture."

"Which is?" I prompt as Jace props himself on an elbow to play with a strand of my hair.

"This isn't an easy lifestyle." Jace's expression borders on melancholy as he twirls the hair between his fingers. "Not everyone believes it's possible to be in love with two people at once, and in a town this small we won't exactly fade into the background."

"I love this town," Blake says to the ceiling. "And the people are some of the best around. But that doesn't mean there won't be talk. I doubt it'd be malicious, but we'll definitely raise some eyebrows. At least to start. Are we all ready for that?"

Blake rolls to his side, mirroring Jace so he can see both of us, although I know he's really talking to me. Am I ready to be the topic of conversation? Probably not. But I have to trust that the three of us together can handle anything the outside world throws at us.

I take a fortifying breath and meet Blake's wary gaze. "I'm ready."

Chapter 28

Blake

This is it. Our first outing as a throuple—or whatever Jace calls it. I'm still not convinced it's actually a term, but whatever. The three of us are solid, and that's all that matters.

To be honest, while I'm ready to take this step, I don't love the idea of going out the day after we got outed. I'd rather enjoy our new relationship just the three of us, because there's no one else I want to see right now. But that would be perceived as hiding, which will only fuel baseless rumors. Stuff like one of us was cheating on the other, which couldn't be further from the truth. That's why we decided to face things head on.

The Underground isn't overly crowded when we arrive, so we find a booth in the corner—not hiding exactly—but not putting ourselves on display, either. We all sit on one side, saving the other for Axel and Lennon, who are going to join us in a show of support. That's not really necessary, but I appreciate it all the same, even if it did take coming out of the closet to get Lennon to take an unplanned night off.

Sandwiched between Jace and Becca I'm actually feeling calm, despite being acutely aware of the not-so-subtle glances boring into the back of my head.

"Nervous?" Jace clasps my thigh under the table.

"Only in the sense that some people might be offended I didn't come out sooner." Small towns are a lot like family in the sense that they always want to know what's going on, and can feel slighted when they don't.

"You think they'll object?" Becca lays her hand on my arm.

"I think they'll have trouble wrapping their heads around it at first, which I think is pretty natural considering I did the same thing. Especially my friends, who never knew I'm into guys, too. I don't think they'll object, though." I chew on my lip as I try to imagine how the night will go.

A pitcher and several glasses banging on the table pulls me out of my head. "How are the local celebrities doing?" Axel shoots Jace a playful wink.

"Don't be a dick." Jace flicks him off.

"I'm not." Axel holds his hands up innocently. "You three are the talk of the town, how are you handling it?"

"The talk is behind our backs." I jerk my head over my shoulder. "You tell us how we should handle it."

Lennon cocks her head to the side thoughtfully. "Well, half the people are saying they knew all along..."

"No surprise there," I mutter. "Nona likes to believe she knows everything, and I'm sure her friends are claiming the same."

Lennon shoots me a wry smile. "Exactly. The other half are surprised they didn't pick up on it since you never really had a girlfriend or whored yourself out like Cade used to and Deacon still does. And everyone, including the two of us," she gestures between herself and Axel, "want to know if they make beds big enough for three people."

Becca chokes on a sip of beer and Jace chuckles while I wipe a hand down my face.

"Seriously, do they? I bet Leni and I could make good use of a bed that big." Lennon rolls her eyes. "What?" He shrugs innocently. "Tell me you wouldn't have fun breaking that in."

That earns him a swat on the arm, and unfortunately, I don't miss the flare of heat in her gaze that comes with it.

We sip our beers and make small talk for the next hour or so, mostly about the work projects we all have going on. Since we all consider our jobs to be more like play, it's less of a bitchfest and more of a brag session. I'm so engrossed, I totally forget about this being our *big reveal* until I hear Deacon's voice echoing through the room as he orders a round of shots.

"When are they ever gonna get tired of that game?" Lennon groans.

"It *is* pretty funny." Jace faces me, waggling his eyebrows. "How come you didn't try to pick me up with some sexy shots the first time I came through town?"

"Because I tried to pick you up with an offer for a massage instead, which you didn't take me up on by the way."

"I would've if we'd stayed in town." He bites the corner of his lip suggestively. "Did you buy Becca a sexy shot?"

"Actually, I picked him up." She gives Jace a little half-shrug when he gapes at her.

"You both picked me up in that bar. Best two nights of my life, until you both moved here permanently." I sip my beer while astonished looks zing around the table.

"Wait – are you saying we picked you up back-to-back? As in the three of us narrowly missed each other in Utah?" Jace's mouth drops open.

I press my lips in a straight line to hold in my grin.

Becca leans forward to see Jace. "Did you know he was that easy?"

Jace looks me up and down slyly. "Manwhore. Are we sure we want to claim this guy as ours, Becca?"

She taps a finger on the corner of her lip as she pretends to mull that over. "I'm sure." She leans in to give me a shy kiss on the lips.

"Okay, fine. Me, too." Jace tugs my head towards his and presses his lips to mine, soft and reassuring. Before we break away a hand slams down on the table, shaking the glasses and causing us to jump apart.

"So, it's true?" Ryder half-shouts, half-slurs. "What other secrets are you keeping from me, Blake? You're the one who broke Chase's heart and forced him to move away, aren't you?"

My jaw hangs open as I blink my eyes, trying like hell to make sense of what he's saying. "What?"

"Admit it. You preyed on him then screwed him over. He moved away so he wouldn't have to see you everywhere."

Holding my hands up in surrender, I hold Ryder's cloudy gaze. "I have no idea what you're talking about, Ryder. I've never been with Chase. He was like a brother..."

"Don't you say that," he sneers. "He was *my* brother, not yours. And you drove him away. It took years, Blake. Years for him to get over you. But he did. He found someone and he was finally happy. I backed out of that trip so he could take his new boyfriend. Now he's dead. He never would have moved from Katah Vista if *you* hadn't screwed him over." He thrusts a shaky finger in my face.

I know how messed up Ryder's been since his brother died in that plane crash, so part of me just wants to ignore this rant and chalk it up to his drunken grief. The other part of me wants to defend myself against his totally insane accusations.

"I didn't hook up with Chase, man. I wouldn't. It sucks he got his heart broken, but don't put that on me because I like dudes as much as I like women."

"Then why didn't you help him? You're just like him and you didn't help him. He felt so alone. You should've been there." His voice loses some of its heat as he starts to ramble.

"I would've if I'd known, Ryder."

"How could you not know?"

My hand cramps from how tight I'm fisting it. "Just because I like guys doesn't mean I have some special skill at picking out other guys who feel the same way, especially if they want to keep that private."

"What's up, bro?" Deacon slings an arm around Ryder's shoulder, eyes searching the stunned faces around the table for a clue about what's going on.

"If it wasn't you then who was it? Who broke him and drove him away from his home? You're the only dude in town into other dudes—it had to be you."

Deacon's playful expression turns somber, telling me he must've already known about Chase's boyfriend. He leans his head toward Ryder and talks to him in a level tone. "Ryder, think about this man. Blake wasn't with your brother. He isn't who you're mad at."

"He has to be," Ryder slurs. "He has to be." He points a finger at me before spinning from Deacon's hold and bolting for the door.

Once Ryder's gone, all eyes turn to me. "I had no idea Chase was gay, and I have no idea who he might've dated. If I'd known, I would've tried to help him."

Lennon reaches across the table and takes my hand, giving it a gentle squeeze. "You don't have to explain anything Blake. We all know

Ryder's in a weird place right now. He's angry at everyone, mostly himself, and is lashing out."

"I knew he was struggling." I drop my head in shame. "I should've been there for him, but I was too wrapped up in my own stuff."

Regardless of the things happening in my life, I should've been more aware of this. His brother is dead, for God's sake, and instead of helping him through that I've been living my life to the fullest, working my dream job and falling in love twice over. I may not have been the one to drive Chase away, but I can't blame Ryder for being pissed at me now.

"We all knew he was struggling, I just don't think any of us realized how bad." Deacon glances toward the door Ryder disappeared out of. "Drowning his feelings seemed natural given the circumstances, but maybe..." He ducks his head and rubs it awkwardly.

"Should I go after him?" I look around the table for input.

"It's probably best if I do that. No offense." He offers me a weak smile.

"None taken." I exhale heavily. "Go."

No one's in the mood to hang out after Ryder's outburst, so we thank Axel and Lennon for the night and make our way back to my place. *Our* place. Climbing into bed with Becca sandwiched between me and Jace.

"So," she drawls as we get comfortable. "*Do* they make beds for three?"

God, I love her for trying to lighten things up. "Are you feeling crowded in my California King?"

"Not at the moment. But I've only stayed over once and that's not enough time to form an opinion. I guess I could always sleep at my place if you two are bed hogs."

Jace shoots upright, staring down at Becca with a pained expression. "You're gonna keep your place? I was sorta thinking you'd move in with us."

Becca's cute little lips form a surprised 'o.' "It's not too soon for that? I mean, we only just made things official."

"Pretty sure in our circumstance there isn't any particular roadmap to follow." I link my fingers with hers. "We'd love to have you move in, but if you want to ease into things that works, too."

Jace is still frowning, signaling he doesn't like that idea, but I'm determined that she make the call on this. We owe her that.

"I mean, employee housing is convenient at all, but it's not really home, you know?"

"This is home," Jace insists.

"Yeah. I kind of think it is." She gives him a shy smile before turning to look at me. "So, a bed for three? And do we each have an assigned spot, or do we rotate? Just because I'm the girl doesn't mean I want to sleep bitch all the time."

Wrapping a hand around her neck, I pull her to me and slap a lingering kiss on her lips. "I love you." I grin. Then I lean up and do the same to Jace. I fall asleep knowing that while fate may have knocked me around a bit to get me to this place, it led me to the future I was meant to have, just like I always knew it would. And it was definitely worth the wait.

***

Ryder

"Ryder Vohrees," The judge's voice echoes through the high ceilings of the courtroom. "You've been charged with one count of driving under the influence. How do you plea?"

My lawyer's face is expressionless as he gives me a curt nod, and I parrot the words he drilled into my head during our last meeting. "No contest, Your Honor."

I'm guilty as fuck–we all know it, thanks to the breathalizer they gave me. Apparently, pleading no contest is like accepting punishment without admitting guilt. I think it's supposed to look better on my record or something, as if I give a shit what my record says. If I gave a shit about anything these days, I wouldn't be in a court, awaiting the inevitable clink of handcuffs being locked around my wrists.

"Very well. I hereby sentence you to one hundred hours of community service. You will report..."

"If I may, Your Honor," my attorney interrupts.

Based on the deep lines between the judge's eyes, I get the impression he *may not*, but that doesn't stop the guy on my left from plowing ahead.

"Carter Quinn would like to propose Ryder perform his community service at the Katah Vista resort." My attorney waves a hand in Carter's direction. "They have an adaptive program for disabled riders, and they are in need of instructors."

What the fuck? This was not part of the plan. I did not plead no contest to get stuck back in the absolute last place I want to be.

I glance over my shoulder to the only other guy wearing a suit here, besides my lawyer. In a manner of speaking, Carter's sort of my boss. His resort is my biggest sponsor, and without him I wouldn't be able to compete on the snowboard circuit. But he already bailed me out of jail when my parents called him in a panic after my arrest, so it'd make more sense for him to drop me than to do it again with this community service gig. *What is he playing at?*

"Is that correct, Mr. Quinn?" The judge arches a thick brow in Carter's direction.

"Yes, Your Honor. Our program is just getting off the ground, and I'm sure you're aware of Ryder's expertise on a snowboard. His experience would be invaluable."

"What experience?" My attorney shoots me a warning glare–I'm not supposed to talk unless I'm asked a question or I risk being out of order or in contempt or something–but speaking up is the only way I can see to stop this train wreck, even if it gets me in more trouble. "I don't know how to teach disabled riders."

"You will once you complete the training program," Carter replies without missing a beat.

I open my mouth again but can't get any words out before my attorney clasps my forearm in his iron grip. *He's stronger than I expected for a suit.*

"Your mission would seem to meet the requirements for community service, but as it's not yet recognized by this court, I'm reluctant to grant this request, even in light of Mr. Vohrees's reputation on the snow." I breathe a sigh of relief as the judge puts an end to my nightmare. *My celebrity isn't going to get me any special favors. Good.* It's short lived.

"I could really use Ryder's help, Your Honor," Carter appeals. "I'll personally oversee his hours to ensure compliance with any instructions you have, and perhaps with the successful completion of our program, will be recognized by the court going forward."

My jaw is locked so tight I think my teeth might crack. I'd rather go to jail than strap on a snowboard. As it is, I get fucking chest palpitations when it snows.

"Seeing as how Mr. Vohrees is a very capable rider, and this is his first offense, your idea has merit. Very well, Mr. Quinn, Mr. Vohrees is in your charge." The judge bangs his gavel, and the courtroom starts to clear out.

"Stay out of trouble." My attorney pats me on the back and stuffs a bunch of papers in his briefcase before heading out the door, leaving me alone in the room with Carter. *Great.*

"You didn't have to do that." I ask him what his deal is without asking outright.

"No, I didn't." The asshole doesn't elaborate.

"Is this how you want me to pay you back for the bail money? Indentured servitude?"

"You don't owe me bail money."

I ball my fists at my sides, seething. "Then why the hell put me on the mountain with a bunch of people I have no business working with?"

"Because you have more business on the mountain than anyone I know." He casually picks his jacket up off the bench, his voice way too calm for my liking.

"I doubt that considering I need special training for whatever you have in mind," I snort.

"The training isn't for what to do on the mountain, it's for what to do with your mouth. Ideally, it will prevent you from saying the wrong thing to the wrong person, like you did with the judge earlier." His brows disappear underneath his hair, daring me to object.

"I know what you're doing. And it won't work." Court order or no, I'm not getting back on that mountain. He should know by now I'm a bad investment.

Carter's eyes roam over me, calculating. "We'll see." He spins toward the door, pausing before he pushes it open. "Be at my office by nine a.m. tomorrow for training. You have two days to complete it before you report to Hailey on Thursday, and trust me when I say you don't want to piss her off."

"Who the fuck is Hailey?"

"Your new manager."

If I wasn't shooting daggers at him I might've missed the wicked gleam in his eye as he saunters out the door. He thinks he's won? That a ballsy chick will make a difference? *Bring it on, boss.*

***

If you enjoyed this story please leave a review. Click here for a bonus scene with Blake, Becca and Jace.

Want more from the town of Katah Vista? Blake never set out to hide who he is, but there's no denying his life is easier with his secrets buried. Find out what happens when Ryder is forced to face his demons in Absolution. Visit my website www.mlenardromance.com and sign up for my newsletter to receive updates on my next series.

The Elevation Series

Distraction

Validation

Revelation

Liberation

Absolution

Exception

You can also check out my contemporary romances in Mile High Romance, a collection of steamy stories about finding love when your career sometimes gets it the way. Set in Denver, Colorado, this series features sports, workplace and forbidden romances, with a flawed yet lovable "relationship whisperer" who is surprisingly good at offering advice that he doesn't know how to take, until its his turn to fall hard.

Books in the Mile High Romance series

Not So Friendly Intent

Purely Novel Intent

Totally Inevitable Intent

Willfully Malicious Intent

Thoroughly Innocent Intent

Strictly Forbidden Intent

For the latest updates on other releases join my VIP reader group.

Acknowledgments: Thanks to my critique group, Janie and Amanda, without whom I wouldn't be whole. You two have challenged me as a writer, and helped me improve my meager design skills. Cover design by Sweet N Spicy Designs.